BREAKING BEAUTY

STELLA ANDREWS

Copyrighted Material
Copyright © Stella Andrews 2020
Stella Andrews has asserted her rights under the Copyright, Designs and Patents Act 1988 to be identified as the Author of this work. This book is a work of fiction and except in the case of historical fact, any resemblance to actual persons, living or dead, is purely coincidental.
All rights reserved. No part of this book may be reproduced or transmitted in any form without written permission of the author, except by a reviewer who may quote brief passages for review purposes only.

18+ This book is for Adults only. If you are easily shocked and not a fan of sexual content then move away now.

NEWSLETTER

Sign up to my newsletter and download a free book

stellaandrews.com

BREAKING BEAUTY

Everyone deserves a second chance – don't they?

Sebastian Stone - the boy I grew up with.

My best friend who I confided in and trusted more than anyone.

The boy who stuck up for me at school and filled my days with laughter and happiness.

The boy who turned into a man who slipped into my bed at night and made me into a woman while the rest of the house slept.

He awakened feelings in me I never knew I had and promised never to leave me.

In return I gave him my innocence and his kisses brought new life to a soul I had surrendered to the Devil many years ago.

However, this sleeping beauty woke up to find her Prince was a monster in disguise because he turned his back on her and chose her sister instead.

When I heard they were to marry I left and fell down the darkest rabbit hole I could find.

But now I'm back and he won't like what I've become. He's about to learn this Princess went over to the dark side and now the only thing on her mind is revenge.

It's time to face my past and change the future - the hard way.

CHAPTER 1

ANGEL

I can't breathe. I thought I was ready to face them again but the fact I'm gasping for air tells me it's still there. The fear. It's why I ran and why I stayed hidden for so long.

"Is everything ok, miss?"

His words have the desired effect and act as a good hard slap in the face as they bring me to my senses.

"I just need a minute."

I swear I can hear my heart thumping because there is silence in the cab as the driver recognizes my need for a moment. If only that was all I needed - a moment. However, that moment turned into weeks, then months, and finally years. Five years, in fact, because that's how long I've been away. I ran to escape them and now I've run right back because the body that waits outside the little white church brought me back to face a past that should have remained there.

Swallowing hard, I take a deep breath and say in a shaky voice, "How much do I owe you?"

"On the house."

He turns and throws me a curious look, and I see the questions in his eyes that I know he will never ask. He smiles kindly and reveals a gold encrusted smile as he says gently, "It's been paid."

Once again, I battle the tears as I nod and say in a voice that sounds nothing like mine, "Thank you."

I don't ask who paid because I already know the answer. My family paid and not the one that's crowded inside that little white church. My real family, the ones who found me and took me in. The people who took a broken angel and built her into the strong woman I am today because I *am* a strong woman. I have become a warrior, a fighter and a woman that takes no shit because of them. Now I need to prove that I've learned the lessons they taught and face my biggest fear.

Taking a deep breath, I take the fire that's been burning inside for what feels like my whole life and caress it gently. It no longer hurts because that fire is what gives me strength. It burns with passion and purpose and is what keeps my cold heart warm and alive. Now I'm going to take that fire and unleash it on the very people who made my life hell and watch them burn in its unforgiving flame.

It's time.

I exit the cab and am relieved to discover my legs hold me in place. Upright and with a strength I thought had deserted me. I steel myself to look at the walnut polished casket and feel a stab of remorse for the man who lies inside. My father.

I see the curious looks of the men who stand by silently, waiting to carry him inside, and the priest smiles at me with a sympathy that's not needed. I don't mourn the man who breathes no more. I don't mourn the fact I never got to say goodbye, and I don't mourn the fact my father is dead.

It's about time.

Pulling my shoulders back, I stare at the men with empty eyes and am grateful mine are hidden behind the blackest shade. The sun beats down on me and warms my soul, and I discover a lightness to my step that fills me with surprise. *I'm ok.*

As the realization hits me, I breathe out in relief. Yes, Angelica Johnson is actually ok. I forgot who she was for a while because I haven't used my full name since I left. I'm Angel now because Angelica deserved to die. She was weak and pathetic and I have no time for her. Angel is the woman I always wanted to be, and she takes no shit, so I stare at the priest and nod coolly and start the long walk inside.

I ignore the curious looks of the congregation as I walk through the church and hear the whispers that follow me like the coolest breeze as I pass. I stare straight ahead and make no eye contact as I walk with purpose to the front of the church. The organ plays its somber tune and I resist the urge to skip like a carefree girl as I head to where I belong. The front.

I hear the gasps as the fact I'm here at all registers with the many mourners crowded inside and as I reach the front, I see the stone-cold faces of the people who dare to call themselves my family.

"Angelica!"

Her voice is soft and disbelieving, and I stare at her with interest, noting the tears glistening in her eyes and the pallor of a woman shrouded in grief. She's aged a lot and I hope I'm responsible. "Hi, mom."

She sobs as she stands to greet me but I take a step back, reinforcing the fact I have an invisible shield protecting me and drag my eyes to the woman who sits beside her. The anger knots inside my heart as the cool eyes of my sister stare back at me. Just for a moment, we are locked in combat. She appears angry that I'm here, which fills me with pleasure.

She should be angry because by the time I've finished she'll wish I'd crawled away to die so she would never have to face me again.

She turns away and my mother says in a hushed whisper, "Move along and let Angelica sit."

As if by magic, a space appears and I take it without uttering a single word. There will be plenty of time for words later and they will not like the ones I speak because five years is a long time to wrestle with the hurt and pain they caused me and it's time to repay the favor.

As the service begins and the body of my father is laid to rest, I wonder if he ever repented his sins. I feel nothing as I listen to the words of a man who obviously didn't know what a monster the Grim Reaper has claimed.

The Grim Reaper, how that name brings joy to my heart and a warm feeling inside. Reaper. Yes, that's what I am now. A Twisted Reaper because when Angelica Johnson was broken, they took her in and put back the pieces with stronger glue. Angel sits among her family as a Twisted Reaper, and they are about to discover what that means.

I know I don't have long. As the service continues, I hear no words spoken. I can't even focus on the fact that I'm surrounded once again by my family because now there is only one thing on my mind. Him.

I stare straight ahead because I can't risk catching sight of the man who broke me. I know he's here. I can feel him. He's sitting a few feet away and yet I haven't laid eyes on him. I know he's here because there's a prickle of electricity that is crackling between us. My heart is twisting inside me as it struggles to remain intact because one look into his eyes and all the good work I've done in keeping myself from folding would be undone in a heartbeat. Even thinking his name sends me into a downward spiral as I imagine how I will feel when I look into those eyes again.

Sebastian Stone. His name causes the oxygen to freeze in my lungs and my heart starts beating a different tune as I contemplate meeting the man who ruined me and I almost run again—almost.

I know he's here because, as I said, I *feel* him. I always have and probably always will.

It's him I focus on getting me through this service. It's him I consider as my father is honored with words and it's him I came back to face. My sister's fiancé.

CHAPTER 2

ANGEL

The service ends and the circus continues outside. As soon as the casket passes me, I'm on my feet and walking purposefully behind it. I stare at nothing as I pass the whispers that follow me wherever I go. I can't make eye contact with the man I now hate with a passion that has only intensified over the years. Love and hate are a double-edged sword because one is never far from the other. I loved him once with my whole heart and that night, like a cancer, hate turned that love into a festering wound that has never healed. It has seeped into the cracks of a broken heart and mind and sown the seed of the greatest hatred a woman can ever feel for a man who took her innocence and crushed it to dust.

As we form a circle around the open pit that will be my father's eternal home, I raise my eyes and stare straight into the ones I fear the most.

He stands across the gaping hole directly in front of me, and I know that was not by chance. He leaves nothing to chance and never has. He has placed himself in my direct line of sight for a reason. He is angry, but I doubt not half as much as I am.

Grateful for the dark shades that obscure my emotion, I stare at the man who caused me to run in the first place. Cold, hard eyes stare back at me with the promise that this isn't over until he says it is.

I feel my heart beating as everything else fades out around me until it's just us, as it always used to be.

Time has been good to him, as I always knew it would. The sharp suits he wears may as well be spun with gold because I can tell his tailor is a costly one. Dark hair as black as the shadows he wrapped me in, gleams in the sunlight and those eyes. They search my soul and rip the answers from inside me with no words spoken. They question and challenge and I swallow hard. Yes, Sebastian Stone grew into an impressive man, and any desire I had for that man was replaced with a white-hot fury and a thirst for revenge.

As the priest commits my father's body to the ground, I commit my soul to revenge. I watch my sister stand beside the man that should have been mine and see her hand on his arm as she stares at me across the divide. The physical and emotional one as we are locked in combat over one man. *Him.* I wonder about their relationship because where she seeks reassurance from him; he offers none in return. She may as well be an irritating insect for all the attention he is showing her. He hasn't taken his eyes off me and there is so much tension in the air I wonder if the oxygen can battle through it.

Then the service ends and we are invited to say our goodbyes. My mother steps forward and places a single white rose on the coffin of her husband and wipes away a lone tear. Mirabelle Johnson. Even now she is keeping up the pretense of actually loving the man inside that coffin, but I know inside, she is probably already planning his replacement. We are taught to love our parents but, in my book, love is earned, not expected, and any I had for that woman died years ago.

She moves away, feigning grief, as my sister steps forward. Anastasia Johnson, bitch sibling from hell. She lies her own white rose on the casket and makes a show of sobbing and stumbling as if in grief. She half turns toward *him*, but he either doesn't notice or ignores her. Who am I kidding, of course he notices, but that's just him, a cold hard bastard with no feelings? I should be glad I had a lucky escape. I should pity my poor sister and I shouldn't care—but I do. I always have done and now, seeing him again, all the work of the last five years counts for zero because as I look into the cold, hard eyes of the man who broke my heart, I am destroyed all over again.

One by one the mourners lay their roses on the coffin of the man who can't hurt me anymore. As they file away, only two people are left standing, Sebastian and me. I know we are providing a freak show for the mourners who are more interested in the power play between us than the fact they've come to pay their last respects to a man who demanded that respect in life but I will not play into their hands. Stepping forward, I ignore the rose with my name on it and grab a handful of dirt from the pile that sits next to the grave and, in full view of everyone, I spit on it and then toss it onto the flower festival covering the wooden box. The gasps echo around the churchyard as I turn and walk away.

I almost make it back to the cab but feel a hand on my shoulder and a familiar voice say angrily, "Angelica, please, just stop!"

Spinning around, I see my mother staring at me with white-hot fury in her eyes and something I'm not prepared for - love.

"Please - don't go."

She reaches up and removes my shades and stares into

my eyes and her voice trembles as she pleads, "Please don't leave again. We need to talk."

If she was hoping to see anything other than hatred in my eyes, she will be disappointed because I face her with twenty-three years of hurt and pain in mine, as I utter the first words I have spoken to her in five years. "Why should I?"

She shrugs and I see a little of her old fire return as she shakes her head. "I know you're angry, but we can talk about that. I just want the conversation that should have happened five years ago."

"A conversation, are you kidding me?"

"Yes, there's a lot that needs to be said and you will hear me out before you head back to god only knows where you've been hiding since you turned your back on this family."

She wants words but they fail me now as she looks at me with the eyes of a woman who never really sees what's staring her in the face. She never did and obviously that hasn't changed.

She smiles and says in a gentler voice, "I know you're angry, but we need to talk about it. Please, come back to the house, just to talk, nothing more. I've missed you so much and can't bear the thought of you walking out on me again."

I half turn toward the cab and she says with some urgency, "Please, Angelica, I'm begging you, don't walk away."

As I turn, I see out of the corner of my eye my sister glaring at me as she watches us. She would like nothing more than to see me disappear again and for that reason alone I say in a harsh voice, "Fine. A conversation it is then."

Mom sighs with relief, and I wonder why she's bothering. She never did all the time I was growing up, so I wonder what's changed? My curiosity wrestles my better judgment as I turn toward the cab. "I'll see you back at the house."

As I slam the door on my mother, I sink back on the seat, close my eyes and take a deep breath. I made it through.

The cab driver turns and says softly, "Where to, darlin'?"

I reel off the familiar address and he turns the engine on and as we pull away, I don't look back. Maybe I never should because what will that solve? Is it worth my time looking back on a past that almost destroyed me? Maybe I should never have come because I am opening a wound that never really healed. Seeing them again reinforced that. Then there's *him* - the boy I grew up with. My best friend and the person I confided in the most. The boy I told my secrets to and trusted more than anyone. The boy who stuck up for me at school and filled my days with laughter and happiness. The boy who turned into a man who slipped into my bed at night and made me into a woman when the rest of the house slept. The man who awakened feelings in me I never knew I had and the man who promised never to leave me. I gave him my innocence, and his kisses brought new life to my soul. However, this sleeping beauty woke up to find her Prince was a monster in disguise because that bastard turned his back on her and chose her sister instead.

The pain stabs me in the heart, as it's always done. I have an invisible knife that set up residency there and twists every so often, reminding me of the pain I felt when I found out the truth.

The tears burn behind my eyes as the past threatens to unravel me again, but I take that pain and form it into an emotion worth hanging onto. Hatred. Seeing them today has revealed that nothing has changed. The last five years have just blurred the picture temporarily because now that picture is back in focus and sharper than ever and now - it's payback time.

CHAPTER 3

ANGEL

The cab pulls into the drive of the house I grew up in. As I look at the impressive façade of a house designed to impress, I feel—nothing. It surprises me because I have come to associate this house with every bad memory in my life and thought it would scare me. It doesn't.

The driver whistles and says with envy, "Man, some people have all the luck. What I wouldn't give for a house like this."

Leaning forward, I say dully, "I wouldn't give you a quarter for it. I'm guessing your home is richer than this one in all the ways that count. Don't be sucked in by appearances because this house is an empty shell. Only bad memories live here and I would trade your home for mine in a heartbeat."

He looks concerned, and I smile wryly. "Take no notice of me, I'm just a bitter shell of the woman I once was."

I see a genuine concern in his eyes as he says softly, "Then why don't we just head back the way we came and save yourself the trouble?"

"Because trouble is something I no longer fear. I've spent many hours dealing with trouble since I left and the woman I am now is very different to the one who walked out those doors five years ago. If you feel sorry for anyone, save your pity for the people who live here - not me. I've moved on and this…" I wave my hand dismissively around me. "Means nothing to me anymore."

He nods and turns to take a last look before starting the engine. "Well, darlin', when you're ready to leave, just call. No charge."

I smile. "No charge, huh?"

"Well, I wouldn't want to mess with a woman like you. Now that would be pretty foolish of me, wouldn't you say?"

He winks and I laugh for the first time in what now seems like years. "You're a wise man…"

"Richie."

"A wise man, Richie. I doubt these people are so wise and it will be fun educating them."

As I step from the cab, he calls, "Hey!"

I turn to face him and he says cheekily, "It was a pleasure darlin' and if you need a place to stay…."

"Thanks for the offer, honey, but I think I'm fine and dandy."

Grinning, I turn away and refocus on the job in hand and as the car makes the steady progress back down the driveway, I head toward the past and all its bitter memories.

Before I even raise a hand to ring the large bell, the door opens and I see a familiar face looking at me with pure emotion. Swallowing hard, I say brightly, "Martha, it's good to see you."

Martha Edwards is our housekeeper and the only woman I love inside these walls. The tears splash onto her beaming face and she envelops me in a huge hug, reminding my senses what a good person smells like. Martha always smelled of cookies and lemon. Don't ask me why, but there was always that comfort in both the woman herself and the smell that surrounded her.

Pulling back, she wipes her tears away and pulls me inside. "I'm so sorry for your loss, Angelica."

"I've lost nothing, Martha, nothing important, anyway."

She shakes her head and looks sad. "It's not right. He was still your father."

"In name only, Martha, you know that."

I look around and see that nothing has changed and feel the walls closing in on me. All around are the memories crowding to the surface to weaken my resolve. I hear his loud, angry voice booming through the walls and shiver a little. Martha takes my arm and says kindly, "Your old room is just how you left it, although I do make up the bed with fresh linen and clean every week. Nothing has changed there."

I take a look at the woman who appears to be the only one that cares and say in a kinder voice, "I've missed you, Martha."

She flushes and I can tell my words mean everything to her. "I've missed you too, dear. This house lost its sunshine the day you left."

Shrugging, I say sadly, "It was always a dark place to me, Martha."

The sound of cars pulling up outside concentrates our minds and Martha looks worried. "They're back, I should get back to the kitchen."

She hurries away, leaving me to walk steadily up the large staircase toward the room that was both my sanctuary and prison combined—my bedroom.

When I head inside, it strikes me that nothing has changed. Looking around the room I knew so well, I could close my eyes and remember every small detail. It surprises me that I feel nothing as I look at my past preserved so well in the present. The girl who lived here is nothing like me. She was scared, vulnerable, and trusting. She believed adults when they spoke their lies and she never thought anything could hurt her.

Walking across to the window, I run my fingers over the glass pane. It feels like yesterday that *he* first visited me here. Sebastian would throw stones at my window in the dead of night and then climb the trellis, and I let him in. At first, we would talk and plot our next escapade. Then, as the years passed, we enjoyed a different kind of relationship.

My heart starts beating as I remember the first time we took our relationship all the way. I had just turned eighteen and that night we both knew it was time.

As I sit back on the bed, I remember how I felt that night. I wanted it so badly and I wanted it to be him. It was always *him*. Even then, he was in control. Just two years older than me but so experienced.

"Angelica, are you in here?"

My mind is brought back to the present as my mother stares at me from the doorway, looking concerned. Nodding, I sit back against the pillows as she ventures in, looking as if she'd rather be anywhere than here.

"It's good to see you where you belong."

"Is it?" I shrug off her comment and face her with a frozen expression.

Sighing, she sits beside me and, as the bed dips, it reminds me of the last time she sat here. That night - the night my world collapsed forever.

Clearing her throat, she says tentatively, "I'm glad you came. It's what he would have wanted."

I feel my chest constrict as she mentions my father. "I expect he would."

Either she doesn't notice the coolness to my tone, or she chooses not to acknowledge it because she laughs softly.

"You know, he never gave up wishing you would return. I know he hired many private investigators to find you, but they never did. Why is that?"

I shrug. "Because I didn't want to be found."

"But why, Angelica? Surely we could have talked it through."

"You think?"

"What's that supposed to mean?"

Feeling the bitterness return, I snap, "Because nobody in this family ever listened to me, so why should that be an exception? What I wanted didn't matter. It was always what *he* wanted for the good of the family. He was prepared to sacrifice his own daughter's happiness for self-gain and I will never forgive him for that."

She takes a deep breath and says in a cold voice, "You're emotional, there's no talking to you when you're like this."

I say nothing because what's the point? We've been over this a million times before and she will never understand me.

She takes my silence as her cue to carry on right where we left off and smiles brightly. "Anyway, none of that matters because you're home now. I'm sure over the weeks we will learn what happened when you left but now, we must send your father off in style."

She stands and holds out her hand, which I pointedly ignore. Looking slightly put out, she hisses, "Don't be difficult, Angelica, you owe it to your father to honor his memory. Now, join me downstairs and do your duty. If anyone asks, we'll tell them you've been traveling around Europe to educate your mind."

She looks at me critically and shakes her head. "Maybe you should change. Your clothes are still in your closet and I don't think the length of your skirt is strictly appropriate for a funeral. Shall we say downstairs in ten?"

She doesn't even wait for my answer before she heads off, the door clicking shut behind her.

As I stare at the wall, I feel the frustration building as I realize I'm right back where I started. She will never change and it's obvious she wants to brush off the last five years and shut it away in a box never to be opened. Maybe the old Angelica would do just that, but Angel is a very different person, and I didn't come here to pick up where I left off. No, they are about to see that their little girl grew up and when she did, she grew sharp teeth to bite them with.

CHAPTER 4

ANGEL

I don't change. I don't even fix my hair or make-up. Instead, I take one last look at my room and bid it a silent farewell. I won't be back, not willingly, anyway.

As I click the door shut on the past, I walk toward the present. I hear the hum of voices below me as I descend the large, impressive staircase. I pass the family portraits that sneer at me, and I battle against the scent of polish as I hold the wooden handrail.

Feeling my heart thump with every step I take, I move toward the door to freedom.

I recognize a few faces, mainly associates of my fathers and don't acknowledge their curious looks and insincere smiles. Luckily, my mother and hated sister are nowhere to be seen, so I walk with purpose to the door and almost make it before a hand grasps my arm and a quivering voice says, "Miss. Angelica, may I have a private word?"

Looking in the direction of the voice, I see a small, ancient looking man, wearing a black suit with a white shirt and black tie. His hair is combed to disguise the bald patch on his head, and his eyes shine behind a small pair of spectacles. He clears his throat. "Allow me to introduce myself. I'm Mr. Featherstone, your father's attorney, God rest his soul."

I say nothing and he says rather firmly, "May I have a word before you leave?"

Feeling a little curious, I nod and follow him into my father's den, which leads off from the entrance hall. As the door closes, I look around and feel the pain return as memories of my father surround me. Dark wood paneling clings to the walls and a large antique looking desk dominates the room. Bookcases stand proudly to attention, crowded with ancient looking books that I swear he never once read. You see, everything in this room was chosen for appearances. Maximum effect to make it look as if he was an educated man - he wasn't. He was just lucky and spent the rest of his miserable life trying to appear more respectable than the crook he really was.

Taking a deep breath, I try to hold it together a little longer and face Mr. Featherstone. "How may I help you?"

He looks a little worried and shakes his head. "This is most unusual, Miss. Johnson, but by the looks of it, you were about to leave and I couldn't let you go without telling you."

"Telling me what?"

He clears his throat and fiddles with his tie as he whispers, "That you have been named in your father's last will and testament."

I feel a little surprised because my father never gave me anything other than the roof over my head and his sharp tongue. The attorney shifts uncomfortably. "This is most unorthodox but I implore you to attend the reading of the will."

"When is it?"

My tone is sharp, but I can't help that. I'm struggling and need some fresh air because it feels as if my father is here in this very room.

"Monday, 9am sharp, in this room."

"Here?"

I can't believe my luck. So much for a fast getaway. "Yes, it's a delicate matter but I need you to be present because it concerns you, among others, of course."

Sighing, I nod. "Ok, I'll be there."

I turn to leave and he says sharply, "Miss. Johnson..."

He smiles. "It will be worth your while; I can promise you that at least."

I say nothing and leave him standing there because I don't trust myself to speak. Whatever my father has planned in death will not be to my advantage, that I'm sure of. Maybe I should just get out now while I still can because if I know my father, I will regret coming back.

The hallway is empty as I head toward the door and I almost make it before I hear, "You've got a nerve."

I freeze on the spot and dig deep inside myself because I'd know that hideous drawl anywhere. Turning, I return the cool look she shoots me tenfold and sneer, "Look what the cat dragged in."

She rolls her eyes. "I never left, what's the matter, sis, you talking about yourself again?"

Just for a moment, we stare at each other with a hatred neither one of us can disguise. After a few tense seconds she snarls, "Don't let me stop you from leaving, I just wanted to make sure you did."

"And why is that exactly? I have nothing you want and neither do you."

"Are you sure about that? I mean, last time we met, I had something you very much wanted. Shame he didn't want you but that's the luck of the draw."

I feel the rage overpowering my reasoning, but don't give her the benefit of seeing it. Instead, I laugh softly. "From what I saw, he doesn't want you either. Shame really, all that scheming and plotting for nothing. I mean, surely yours must be the longest engagement in history, what's the matter, are you losing your touch?"

I see I've hit a nerve when she hisses, "How dare you come back here and say such vicious lies. Sebastian loves me and can't wait to marry me. You're just jealous because he chose me over you."

Advancing toward her, I snarl, "Are you sure about that? I mean, did he really choose you, or was he *made* to choose you. I think there's a difference and we both know which one really happened."

She raises her hand and I catch it as she makes to slap me hard across the face. As I twist her arm, I relish the pain in her eyes as I sneer, "Look at how pathetic you are. So afraid for her failed relationship you're worried that I'll destroy the last shred of it now I'm back. Well, relax sis because I'm not staying and even if I was, I wouldn't want *him*."

Pushing her roughly back, I spin on my heels and head purposefully to the door, and her bitter words follow me. "Keep walking, Angelica, because nobody wants you here, they never did."

Slamming the door behind me, I almost run down the steps and then, as I reach the bottom, I could kick myself. I left my purse inside, along with my cell. Great, now what?

CHAPTER 5

ANGEL

I just can't face going back inside. Coming here at all was a huge test in itself and I need to leave before the shell I've protected myself in proves it's not as hard as I thought it was.

Instead, I make my way around the side of the house to where I know I'll be safe, the kitchen.

As I walk, I note that nothing has changed since I left. The flower borders are still weed free and manicured to the point of ugliness. I've grown to hate the perfection that man deems beautiful. To me it's ugly and false. True beauty is in the most barren of landscapes. A lone plant clinging to life against the elements. Beauty can flourish in the hardest of places and that is, as its name suggests, the purest form of beauty. This contrived perfection sickens rather than pleases and I feel the stench of the past returning to suffocate me as I try not to look as I pass. By the time I reach the kitchen, I feel nauseous and just pray that Martha is the sole occupant.

Peering through the window, I see her working away as she's always done. God only knows why she stays because surely, she would have a better life anywhere but here, but she's loyal and I know would never leave my family. I tap gently on the window and she looks up sharply. A smile breaks across her face as she sees me peering in and she looks around her before heading across to the door. "Angelica, what are you doing out there?"

"Listen Martha, I need your help."

She smiles and I don't miss the curiosity in her eyes as I say quickly, "I've left my purse on my bed and wondered if you could fetch it. I'm sorry to ask but I won't go back inside because I can't risk seeing anyone."

I know she feels bad because her face clouds with a pained expression and she shakes her head. "It's not right, Miss. Angelica. You shouldn't be afraid to go into your own home. Come inside and I'll make you a hot drink and we can talk it through."

I feel a little panicked because I need to leave before my resolve crumbles, so I say rather cruelly, "Don't question me, Martha, I just need this one favor - please!"

I try not to feel bad as I see the hurt expression in her eyes. I can't possibly take her up on her kind offer because a bit of kindness goes a long way with me at the moment and I don't want to reveal that I'm way out of my depth here because the thing that scares me the most, is running into *him*, which is sure to happen if I went back inside. In fact, I think I've got off lightly so far and don't want to push my luck, so I plead, "Please, Martha, I'm begging you."

Nodding, she whispers, "Of course. Stay right where you are and I'll be back before you know it."

"No, I'll meet you out the front. I need to be able to make a swift getaway if anyone sees me."

Looking unhappy, she turns away and I breathe a sigh of relief. Thank god, I knew she would understand. She always did.

I make my way around the side of the house, retracing my steps and feel grateful that it's starting to rain. Hopefully, the weather will keep the guests inside, giving me time to get the hell out of here. I don't register that I'm getting wet and I don't care that I'm shivering because it's a small price to pay for freedom.

Standing under a tree to the side of the house, I wait for Martha and as I hear her footsteps approaching, I almost cry with relief. I just need my cell to call the cab, and then I can go to a safe place to consider my options.

However, the person that comes into view makes my heart plummet like a lead weight. The shivers that wrack my body are no longer from the cold and the water on my eyes is not from the rain because, holding my purse and looking so incredibly angry is the one person I never wanted to see again, Sebastian Stone.

I hear the screams in my mind as I face my biggest fear. He prowls toward me like the predator he is, and I can almost taste his anger in the air. He stops a few feet from me and holds out my purse. "Yours I believe."

His voice is deep and husky, as it always was. That voice used to send desire straight to my core because it's the sound of power and of a man who demands respect. However, any respect I ever had for him was destroyed that day, so I step forward and snatch my purse from his hands and turn to walk away.

A hand on my arm stops me in my tracks and as I stumble, that same arm pulls me into a hard body and strong arms lock me in a prison I know I will struggle to free myself from. He leans down and his whisper sends shivers through my body as he says softly, "Going somewhere?"

Just for a moment my defenses are weakened and any smart retort I have been rehearsing for five years is forgotten in a heartbeat as the familiar feeling of being in his arms melts my heart and renders me an idiot. Then the memories resurface along with my anger and I push him sharply away, hissing, "Don't touch me."

The look on his face almost makes me laugh out loud because I've learned a lot in the past five years and my strength is one of them. He stumbles back under the force of my shove, and I face him with my eyes flashing. "I'm sorry, do I know you?"

He nods and I see a weariness in his eyes that tells me everything I want to know. He's unhappy. Well, that makes two of us, so I start to walk away, hoping that he takes the hint and stays put. However, he never could take a hint and I hear his footsteps follow me and he says in a dull voice, "You owe me an explanation at least. Is that too much to ask?"

Stopping suddenly, I spin around and look at him in disbelief. "I owe you nothing. You know, maybe once we were friends. Maybe once I would have owed you something, but not now. You see, the day you turned your back on me and proposed to my sister, I think that pretty much canceled out any debt I ever owed you. In fact, come to think of it, you probably owe me, so fuck off, Sebastian, and run back to the whore you call your fiancée and I hope you'll both be very miserable because you deserve each other. Now if you don't mind, I am a busy woman and only came to check that the bastard who called himself my father is actually dead and buried. Now I can go back to my family and live a happy life without any of you in it."

I turn away before my voice reveals how close I am to breaking and he says, "Family?"

Just one word and yet I hear the many questions loaded in it. His sounds lost and slightly vulnerable, which hurts me way more than it should. Not trusting myself to speak, I carry on walking and as I hear his footsteps walking in the other direction, I feel the tears running down my cheeks in rivers.

I make it out of the gate and onto the road outside where I intend on calling a cab before a car slows down beside me and the window winds down and I hear a voice shout, "Get in."

I carry on walking and completely ignore him because Sebastian is obviously not taking no for an answer. As I walk, he crawls beside me, and just knowing he is so close makes breathing difficult. After a few minutes, I stop suddenly and shout, "Just fuck off and leave me alone! I don't want anything from you."

"Listen, I'm going nowhere, so you may as well jump in. This will be over a lot quicker if you just let me take you where you're heading and then I promise I'll leave you in peace."

Maybe it's because I'm cold and my feet are starting to hurt that I give in so quickly and say angrily, "Fine, but you can take me straight to the cab office in town. I don't want to spend a minute more with you than I need to."

I don't miss the triumphant gleam in his eye as I climb inside the passenger seat and edge as close to the door as possible. Being in such close proximity to the man I ran from is the hardest thing I have ever done, so I stare pointedly away from him and clutch my purse to my chest as if it's a shield that will protect me from him.

I don't miss that he turns the heater on high and feel grateful for the warm jets of air that caress my body breathing new life into it.

I try to focus on the speeding landscape outside as he says softly, "We need to talk—properly."

"I have nothing to say."

"Maybe not but I do."

Shrugging, I say dully, "I don't want to hear it."

As the car eats up the distance, I try to focus on anything other than the situation I'm in and can't believe that I'm here at all. Then, just when I think he's given up and is actually going to leave me alone, he pulls the car to the curb sharply and locks the doors.

CHAPTER 6

ANGEL

Frantically, I try to unlock the door but the bastard obviously has total control of them because he says firmly, "I've waited five years to say what I want to say and you *will* listen."

"I will listen. How dare you. I won't listen to a word you speak from that lying mouth of yours because I know everything I need to already. Did you not agree to marry my sister?"

He nods but I see the fire in his eyes as he snaps, "I had to."

"Had to!" I laugh bitterly. "Well honey, *had to* doesn't cut it. You know, maybe once I would have believed your lies. Maybe once I could have forgiven you for them and maybe once I would have been happy to be locked in this car with you but not now."

"And why is that?"

"Because I've moved on. You see, Sebastian, once upon a time this little princess thought you were her Prince Charming. She believed you when you crawled into her bed at night and spoke about a life filled with happy ever afters.

She was impressed by the man who warmed her heart during the darkest storm and she would have believed anything you said. However, this fairy tale didn't have a happy ending. The wicked king put paid to that and altered everything. I mean, where does it say in the fairy tales that the Prince marries the ugly sister because I must have missed that one? So, whatever you have to say doesn't matter anymore. I have a new life and a new family. People who love me and a place to call home. So, be a good boy and drop me where I want to go because I don't want to hear it."

"Where do you want to go, I'll take you there?"

I feel surprised that he's already given up trying and a little disappointed as I say roughly, "I told you, the cab office in town."

"No, I'll take you home to your—family."

I see his eyes flash and realize he's testing me and I feel the irritation prickling inside as I snap, "If I told you where I lived, I'd have to kill you."

He smirks and I say angrily, "I could kill you, Sebastian, in fact, I'm close to it now."

He is almost laughing as he shakes his head. "And how would you do that, I wonder? Is there a samurai sword in your purse, or a gun perhaps? Hmm, maybe not because that purse looks fit for a handkerchief and nothing more. Maybe you will karate chop me into oblivion or bore me to death because if I remember rightly, you couldn't even punch yourself out of a paper bag."

Just for a moment, I let his words sink in and he turns on the ignition and drawls, "So, come on, Angelica, why don't you take me home to meet your new perfect family?"

I want to smash his head against the window and remove that smirk from his mouth with my fists. I want to head butt him into the afterlife and cut off his balls but instead, I preserve my dignity and say calmly, "The cab office will be fine, thank you."

It surprises me when he nods and pulls away from the curb in the direction of the town. No words are spoken as the car eats up the distance and he even flicks on the music to disguise the awkward silence. I try to relax, feeling astonished that it was so easy. Then, as he pulls into the parking space outside the cab office, I am more surprised that he doesn't stop me from leaving the car.

As I slam the door on the past, I'm not sure of the future. He gave up on me—again. It's what I wanted, wasn't it? As I walk into the cab office, I tell myself I'm glad he did. However, the only person I'm fooling is myself because suddenly it feels as if I've lost him all over again and it hurts like hell.

IT DOESN'T TAKE LONG to book a cab and start the journey to my temporary home. As I reel off the address, the driver looks surprised. "Are you sure, honey?"

"Of course, I'm sure."

He hesitates and then says with a curiosity I'm used to hearing, "It doesn't feel right taking a young girl like you there."

"Maybe not, but it's where I want to go. Why is that so difficult?"

He falls silent, and I know he's concerned. Like most of our safe houses, they are protected by tales of terror that keep everyone away. However, as I sink back in my seat, I can't wait to get there. To get to a place where I feel safe and secure. A place that will allow me space to breathe and work out my next move. I need this time because I can't leave before hearing my daddy's will and I'll need the following days to build up a strength that has been tested so severely today.

As we turn off the main highway down the dusty track, I feel comforted by the bumps over the rough terrain. The trees that line the route offer seclusion and a distance from a civilization that would never understand the life I now live.

The driver interrupts my thoughts and says in a worried voice, "I'm sorry, honey but you should know the same car has followed us the whole way."

"And you're just telling me that now?"

I feel angry because there are no prizes for guessing whose car that is and I say angrily, "I wish you had told me and we could have shaken him. Now he knows where I live and everything's ruined."

The driver shakes his head. "Then whoever's driving is a fool."

"You're right about that."

Once again, the tears threaten to reveal how fragile I am, and I feel the despair overwhelming me. He can't come here; I need to be alone. The trouble is, he knows where I'm going now because this road leads to only one place. Hell.

CHAPTER 7

ANGEL

We draw up outside a wooden cabin in the heart of the forest where the track runs out. The car behind me comes to a halt behind us, but I don't care anymore. He can deal with the consequences of following me by himself because he won't like what he finds.

The driver waves away the dollars in my hand and says fearfully, "On the house."

Placing it carefully on the seat beside me, I say gently, "Thank you, this is your tip."

He makes to speak, and I smile reassuringly. "Please - it will make me happy."

He nods and I can tell he wants to leave as quickly as possible and I can see why, because parked outside the cabin is a beast on two wheels. To everyone else, the emblem on the side promises pain and retribution. It's unforgiving and takes no shit, just like the man who rides it. I'm surprised at who they sent but not unhappy about it. How can I be because he is just the man I want to see right now and I scramble out of the cab, desperate to run into the comfort his arms provide?

The cab doesn't wait to find out and squeals off down the track and I turn to see Sebastian leaning against his hood, watching me with cold, calculating eyes. Before I can even warn him to leave, the cabin door flies open, and I almost weep with relief. "Who the fuck is that, Angel?"

I watch as the blood drains from Sebastian's face as he sees the beast before him. Filling up the doorway is the man who sits on the right hand of Satan himself. His cold, deadly eyes pierce through the darkness and the light from the cabin reveals the monster within. His head is shaven and a huge tattoo of a cobra wraps around his arm to his neck, drawing attention to the huge biceps they decorate. This man takes no shit and could kill us both within seconds, and I have never been so pleased to see him in my life.

He prowls down the steps menacingly and stares at Sebastian with the cold, hard look of a killer before saying roughly, "You have two seconds to get back in your car and leave. Nobody comes here but the invited and you are not one of them, so leave while you still can."

I hold my breath as Sebastian stares at him with an angry expression and I see the fire in his eyes weighing up the situation. Then his better judgment kicks in and without a word gets back into his car and leaves without a backward glance.

As his taillights disappear down the track, I turn to the man who scared him off and run into his arms, sobbing with relief. As those arms of steel wrap around me, I feel everything slot back into place. I'm home.

By the time we get inside, I've composed myself and feel a little foolish. Snake turns to me, and I see the concern in his eyes as he nods toward the couch. "Sit."

My legs fold under me as I sink into the comfort of the

couch and it sags as he sits beside me and places his arm around my shoulders, pulling me into his side where I have sat a thousand times before.

"It's good to see you, Snake."

"You too, darlin'. How did it go?"

"As expected."

"What's that supposed to mean?" I hear the impatience in his voice and laugh softly. "You always were impatient, Snake."

He laughs. "That guy outside, is that him?"

"Yes." My heart plummets as I think about Sebastian and Snake growls, "I should have fucking wasted him - prick."

"He's not worth it."

Spinning around, I raise my eyes. "I'm surprised they sent you. Things must be quiet back home."

"I suppose they are but I would have come, anyway."

"Why?"

"Because we care about you, darlin'. You wouldn't let anyone come and we know how hard this is for you. Ryder wanted me to check you're ok and bring your stuff."

He nods toward the pile of cases in the corner.

"You got those on your bike?"

Laughing, he shakes his head. "No, I brought the truck. It's parked out back and I loaded my bike on board. You need a car, so you can keep that."

"Great, that'll go down well when I rock up to the house on Monday in a pickup. My mom will have a seizure."

"It's a win win then."

We grin at each other, and I lean back and stretch out. "How's Bonnie?"

I watch as Snake's expression softens at the mention of his old lady, and he smiles sweetly. "Studying. She's got her final exams next week and my life is hell."

"I doubt that."

He laughs as I shove him hard. "Just because she's paying you no attention, you're pissed. You guys are all the same. You think the whole world revolves around you but newsflash, it doesn't."

"You sound like Bonnie."

"I've lived with her long enough, it must have rubbed off."

He settles back beside me and says gently, "So, what did you learn?"

His words bring back the horror of my day and I say sadly, "That my old ghosts weren't buried with my father. I saw my mom and felt nothing. Does that make me a bad person?"

"No."

"My sister too; I hate the evil bitch and I feel as if I let myself down when I spoke to her."

"How?"

"Because there was so much I wanted to say and yet I resorted to childish digs. You know, Snake, I wanted to walk in there and prove I was some sophisticated lady who no longer cared what happened in the past. I had images of myself tossing my hair back and being quick witted and cool. I wanted them to see that they hadn't broken me and none of it mattered anymore."

"But it does."

The tears almost blind me as I nod. "Yes, it matters a lot."

"What about the guy, how did you feel when you saw him?"

The pain hits me once again, and my voice shakes. "The same."

He pulls me against him and rubs my shoulder. "I'm sorry, darlin', what you gonna do about it?"

"I don't know." I sigh heavily. "I must stay and listen to my father's will read on Monday. Apparently, I'm named in it.

God only knows what horrors he's dreamed up for me and I wish it didn't matter and I could just walk away but it does."

Snake nods. "You know, darlin', you need to see this through if you stand any chance of healing. When we found you in Stoker's MC and brought you to the compound, you were so brave. We saw the strength in you because after what you went through, you still had fire in your eyes. Over the years I've seen that bravery first hand and know that you can conquer anything, if you want to, that is. I'm guessin' there's unfinished business you need to resolve and you can only make a decision when you have the answers you need."

"But what if I make the wrong one?"

"You won't. You know, Angel, if your path ends here in this town, I'll be happy for you. If it brings you back to The Reapers, I'll be just as happy. We live a fucked-up life that nobody who hasn't lived it can possibly understand. Some of us will never leave and thrive on it. Some leave and find their lives outside the steel walls we live inside. They are still family though, so whatever you choose, know you'll always have a home with us. We're your protection, your backup and your bolt hole. We are always there for you night and day and you only have to call and we'll be there. Do what you have to because the only important thing is to make Angel happy, it always was."

As the tears fall, he takes my hand in his and I squeeze it hard. "Thanks, Snake. I owe everything to you and the Reapers. I'm going to take the next few days to work out where I go from here. The answer may be written on the pages of my daddy's will, but whatever those words say, I know they won't be easy to hear. It's why I wanted to come here alone, because I need a clear mind. When I left all those years ago, I was running. I ran straight into trouble and then I found Stokers MC. It was perfect because I knew my folks would disapprove, hell, they would hate knowing their princess was a biker whore and that's why I went there. I also knew they would protect me from the people I hated, and yet I didn't know what I was getting into. We both know the club was corrupt and you and Ryder took them down, as they always knew you would. When you took me to live with the Reapers, I discovered what family really means. So, thank you, Snake. I can't repay what you and the guys gave me but I need to find out who Angel will be in the future. Maybe living as a Twisted Reaper is what was always meant to be, but I need to bury the past before I can deal with the future."

Snake nods, and I know he understands. Every single member of the Twisted Reaper MC is there for a reason, and most of them bad. Ex-Navy Seals and military, all running from their past. Now paid government assassins doing the establishment's dirty work underneath the radar. Feared and respected in equal measures, they carry out their duties in a blaze of machine gunfire and hard expressions. Nobody messes with the Reapers and they have taught me well.

Turning to Snake, I say in a stronger voice. "You know, I'm glad to see you, honey. You've reminded me of who Angel is. For a moment back there, I lost her but when I attend that meeting on Monday, I will walk in there with her firmly in charge. I know what to expect and will hear the will and then make my decision."

Standing, Snake laughs softly. "Then I can see I am no longer needed. Stay strong, darlin' and call if you need us."

He heads to the door and I call out, "Tell Bonnie and the rest of them I miss them."

"You can tell them yourself when you come to visit."

"Just visit?"

He winks. "It will be interesting to find out."

His laughter follows him through the door, and I grin. Yes, they know me so well and even I know I've made my mind up already. Even if I do decide to stay, they will always be my family and yes, I will most definitely go back. However, it won't be as a resident, it will be as a visitor because I can't hide forever. I need to stand up and make something of my life wherever that ends up to be.

CHAPTER 8

SEBASTIAN

Five long years, two months, twenty-three days and six hours since she left and seeing her again proved it's still there. I knew she would come back for her father's funeral. I was counting on it because if I didn't know already, Angelica took my heart with her that day and still owns it now.

As I reach the highway, I feel a pain so sharp it physically hurts - she's moved on.

That man is proof of that and her ice-cold attitude. I feel sick thinking of her with that... I don't even know what he is because all I saw was a shed load of trouble that looks to belong in an MC club. Just thinking of her in that world makes me want to hurl. Not her. She doesn't belong there. Angelica is and always was a princess. Beautiful long blonde hair, stunning blue eyes the color of crystal waters, a creamy pale complexion like pure porcelain, and an innocence that made everyone who crossed her path fall in love with her, me included. Especially me because growing up alongside her made me fall in love with her more and more every day.

Until *that* day. The day I was given no other choice—marry her sister or face the consequences.

Leaving her back there was a choice that wasn't mine to make. It tore me up to drive away and just thinking of her now with that beast is too much. Then the anger takes over and self-preservation kicks in. She ran, and she didn't even bother to hear why. I thought we were better than that. I thought she would understand, but she never gave me that option. Well, now she's moved on and so must I. Harvey Johnson is dead and I wish it had come sooner. Just thinking about that man leaves a bitter taste in my mouth and encases my heart in ice. He ruined men for fun, and we were no exception. It's why I did what I had to do and now it's time to get my revenge.

I hoped I'd see Angelica today and now I wish she had never returned because far from saving me; she has signed my life sentence. I had hoped that love would conquer all. How naïve I was. Angelica never loved me; it was just childhood infatuation. Now she has proved that we never meant anything at all and I suppose, if anything, it will make this easier.

Rather than drive back to the funeral, I head home instead. I can't face that family tonight; I need to distract myself from what I just saw. Turning the car in the opposite direction, I head to a place I can be the monster I became. Blacks.

As I park the car, I try to ignore the pain that Angelica's return has brought. I've thought of this meeting every day since she left and never imagined it like this. She was so cold, so cool and so sexy it made my head spin. When I saw her enter the church, it took all my self-control not to jump up and drag her next to me where she belongs. Instead, I had to sit through the service, honoring a man we both despised while thinking of her sat a few feet away.

The past five years have counted because during them I paved the way for our future, or so I thought. When I saw what her future looked like, it brought with it a crashing realization that during that time I had lost her.

Pushing away the thought of what that now means for my own life, I push the door open to the only place I can fully relax and feel the calm settle over me as I breathe in the familiar scent of oblivion.

Nodding coolly at the receptionist, I sign in and she smiles. "Good afternoon, sir."

Nodding, I move past and don't even care that I'm being rude. I have no time for polite chit chat. I never did, and that's why this place has become so important to me. It requires none.

As soon as I walk into the bar, I see it's quiet. Maybe it's because it's earlier than normal, but there are only a few couples milling around and I feel irritated. Heading toward the bar, I nod at the bartender. "Double scotch on the rocks."

He nods and sets about fixing me the drink that I hope will dull the pain inside, along with the girl sitting on the barstool looking at me hopefully. As I look at her, she lowers her eyes, and I feel my heart settle a little. Yes, she'll do.

Moving across to her, I say forcefully, "Name?"

"Kitten, master."

I note the tight corset she wears, causing her breasts to spill over the top and take in the fact she wears nothing else but a lace thong. She is pretty enough with long red hair and bewitching green eyes. Her body is enticing and her manner a complete turn on, but today even the thought of indulging in a scene with a random sub doesn't interest me because *she's* back.

Fighting my irritation, I try again.

Reaching down, I lift her face to look at mine and see the excitement in her eyes as she licks her lips with either nerves or suggestion. Running my thumb over her lips, I watch her breathing change as her chest falls rapidly, causing her breasts to swell even more. I search for my own feelings as I feel the soft skin of a woman who, like me, wants to lose herself in the pleasures of the flesh, but the desire I once felt for this kind of activity appears to have deserted me today. Thinking of what I could do to this woman doesn't excite me as it should and if I feel anything, it's anger at my own weakness. Almost apologetically, I pat her head and say softly, "I'm sorry, I'm not staying."

Her lower lip trembles and I feel like a bastard because she probably thinks it's her, and I shake my head. "Maybe next time."

Grabbing my drink, I toss the contents of the glass down in one and head across to a secluded booth. Great, fucking idiot, now what? I can't go home because I'm not one to drink and drive and I could call a cab, but why return to an empty apartment where the emptiness will just highlight my loneliness? I certainly won't return to Angelica's home because the thought of what lies in wait leaves me cold. Anastasia.

Sighing, I settle back against the leather seat and think about the woman I'm engaged to marry. Angelica's sister. Whenever I think of her, I feel the rage twist inside my gut and cause my temper to flare. Why was I so weak?

I should have said no, and I should have fought for the woman I was always meant to marry. Instead, I allowed myself to be corralled into doing what Harvey Johnson wanted because of the good son I was. Now that's got me in a situation I can see no way out of because when I saw that beast waiting for my perfect Angel, I wanted to hurl on the spot. I feel so responsible because it appears I drove her away to a life that no decent girl should live. My perfect Angel is a biker whore, and I almost can't breathe as I think of what that means for her.

A man slides into the booth opposite, and I look up and nod. "Logan."

He smiles and holds out his hand. "Sebastian, it's been a while."

He slides another glass of whiskey across to me and raises his glass to mine. "To old friends."

We tap glasses and as the liquid hits the back of my throat, I relish the burn as it dulls the hurt inside me.

"It's unusual to see you here, Logan."

He nods. "Just checking up on my investment."

He looks at me with interest, and I can tell he misses nothing. "What's up?"

Setting my glass down, I sigh heavily. "Life."

He leans back in his seat. "Do you wanna talk about it?"

"Not really. I thought coming here would help, but it's just made me realize just how fucked up my life is. I can't even get my shit together for a scene with a willing submissive."

"It happens."

"Not to me."

For a moment we sit in silence and then I raise my eyes to his concerned ones and say darkly, "Angelica's home."

"I thought so."

Sighing, I caress the cool crystal of the glass and sigh. "She showed up at the funeral and I thought I was ready. I thought we would have a conversation, and an explanation was all that would be necessary."

"But it wasn't?"

"No. She's moved on, Logan."

"I'm sorry man."

Sighing, I feel the weariness wash over me and as I stare into my future, it's a bleak one without her in it. Leaning forward, I say huskily, "I followed her to a cabin out in the woods. When I got there, she wasn't alone. Some fucking brute of a biker was waiting for her and made it clear I wasn't welcome. I had no other choice but to leave her behind because one look in his eyes told me he was above the law and not afraid to protect what was so obviously his."

Logan looks thoughtful. "Did you see what club he was from?"

"How the fuck do I know, I avoid those bastards like the plague? He had a monster tattoo of a snake covering him and a shaven head if he wasn't frightening enough just from his biceps alone."

Logan begins to laugh, and I feel the anger returning. "What's so funny?"

Shaking his head, Logan grins. "Sounds like you described a person I know and love."

"Are you fucking mad? That man was a beast."

"You're right there, he is, and you did well to leave. It appears that your lady got herself the best protection there is and you're right, it is an MC club. However, not like any we have ever known and if I'm not mistaken brother, she's run straight into the arms of the Twisted Reaper MC and far from feeling angry, you should feel relieved."

"Are you fucking kidding me?"

"No, I'm deadly serious. Listen, Sebastian. I know something about your story and it's not a happy one. When Angelica ran, I know what a shit storm it stirred up. Ask yourself why she's remained so hidden for five years. You told me yourself her father had paid the best detectives to find her and yet they came up empty."

"So?"

"She ran to a place where she would never be found. If she was, no one would ever speak of it if they knew what was good for them. No, my friend, because if she's with them, it changes everything because the fact she's back at all tells me it's not over yet."

"How do you know so much?"

"Because I know the Twisted Reapers and how they operate. That man you saw isn't interested in Angelica, not in the way you think, anyway. I happen to know he is madly in love with an amazing girl of his own and was there for only one reason."

"Which is?"

"Protection. Angelica is obviously under their care and they look after their family. If he was there, it's doubtful she's with anyone because if she was, it wouldn't have been him standing there. So, drink up my friend and plan your next move because your story isn't over yet. Trust me, if I know anything, it's that."

"How come you know them so well?"

"I know a lot of people and some would rather I kept that to myself."

He shrugs and grins wickedly. "You're best staying away until Angelica comes to you because you were wise to leave her behind. Those men are assassins, and death is a job to them. If anything, you should be grateful she found them because she would have been cared for and safe and now my friend, you will have to sit back and wait for the fireworks because if I'm right, there is about to be quite the show."

Logan grins and I feel something return that I thought was lost. Hope.

CHAPTER 9

ANGEL

Snake left, and I spent the weekend trying to get my shit together. I can't shake the image of Sebastian walking away from me—again, and I'm trying not to picture him with my hated sister. Images of them together haunt my dreams and sit on my shoulder as I try to get through the day. Just the sight of him was enough to destroy me all over again and as the hours tick past, my heart hardens around the pain and wraps it in an impenetrable hatred for the people I will have to face on Monday morning.

I don't think I sleep a wink on Sunday night and as I dress for my meeting with my father's attorney; I take pleasure in wearing something completely unsuitable for the occasion.

Smoothing down my short red skirt, I climb onto the highest heels I own. The tight-fitting V-neck sweater clings to my curves, leaving nothing to the imagination. I brush my hair until it forms a blonde cloud around my face and my make-up is bold and alluring, providing a mask for me to hide behind. Yes, Angelica is now a whore, and a good one at that. However, I am no ordinary whore because I receive no money for my services. I seek comfort from the men who protect me in return. The Twisted Reapers are one fucked up band of brothers who are all hiding from something. We live together and take comfort in the fact we are all the same. It's no hardship living in such a candy store. Yes, I enjoy the physical benefits living there offers and I love every minute of it. However, none of them have been able to fill the hole inside me where Sebastian ripped my heart out and kept it the day I ran. As hard as I've tried, I can't erase him from my memory and now I've returned to steal it back again.

I set off in the large pickup truck that Snake left me and laugh to myself as I imagine my mom's horror-stricken face when I rock up in this. I can't wait to see the anger in her eyes as her daughter returns, no longer dressed in respectability. I just hope she's embarrassed because I am what she made me, her and my father and hiding behind the Reapers has given me the courage to face my past.

I turn on the music as high as my ears will allow and sing along to my favorite tunes. Yes, Angel's not Angelica and she has perfected the attitude that will get her through this torture.

∼

MAKING sure to send the gravel flying, I skid to a halt in the driveway and laugh to myself. I can't wait to see the faces of my family when they see what I've become.

Making sure to collect my fuck off attitude, I slam the car door and flick the lock and head toward the huge front door with confidence. When I last came here, I wasn't sure what to expect. Now I know and can deal with it.

Martha answers the door and looks at me in surprise as she takes in my disrespectful attire, and I grin. "Good to see you, Martha; I could murder a coffee."

Shaking her head, she allows me to pass, and I stride into the hallway. "Where are they?"

"In the living room."

I sense the resignation in her voice and throw her a smile. "I'm sorry, Martha."

"For what?"

"For everything you've put up with all these years. It can't have been easy, but you stuck it out. Why is that?"

I watch her eyes fill with tears and she brushes them away. "Because of you and your sister."

"But why?" I feel shocked to see the genuine love in her eyes, and she whispers, "Because I couldn't have children of my own, so I transferred that love over to you and Anastasia. You needed me and I was happy to step up."

Her words have delivered a knockout punch as I see the love shining in her eyes and I think back to a past where she was the constant in our lives. While mom was out playing the lady of the house, Martha adopted her role concerning us. She cooked our meals, played with us, tended us when we were sick and molded us into the women we became. It was Martha who read us stories and listened to our chatter. She watched with delight when we performed our shows and admired the paintings we brought proudly to show her. Martha was the one I turned to when childhood was replaced with the scary prospect of puberty. She was the one who solved our arguments and taught us how to get along. As the fog clears, I see it all, and I can't disguise the emotion her words bring. Yes, if anyone has been like a mother to me, it's this woman standing meekly by my side and I suddenly feel an overwhelming wave of pure love for her. To her surprise, I draw her into my arms and relish the comfort she gives me. Yes, cookies and lemons will always remind me of home because that's where *she* lives.

"Angelica!"

The sharp voice of my mother makes my heart sink and I pull back and note her disapproving stare.

"What on earth are you wearing, go and change at once?"

"No thanks."

"What do you mean, no thanks, how dare you disrespect your father's memory by coming here dressed as a…"

"Whore?" I finish her sentence and relish the way her eyes flash as she hisses, "Yes, a whore. Now go and change at once before I do something I regret."

"Nothing changes then."

She steps back as if my words strike a physical blow. Then I watch her regain her composure as she always does and pulls herself up, snarling, "Don't be facetious. Now do as I say and change. Martha will help you and make sure you are dressed accordingly. You have five minutes so don't dawdle."

She spins on her heels and heads back the way she came, and I poke my tongue out at her childishly. I sense Martha's disapproval and sigh inside. "I'm sorry, Martha, she always brings out the worst in me."

I detect a glimmer of amusement in Martha's eyes as she says gently, "Come, I'll help you find something."

Shaking my head, I make to follow my mother, "No thanks, I'm fine as I am."

I hear her sighing as I walk away and feel a little bad for her. I know I'm being rebellious, which is totally the opposite of what I was growing up, but I don't care. If my family doesn't like Angel then I don't like them—period.

Making sure to fling the door open for maximum effect, I saunter into the room and note with interest the select gathering milling around, talking in hushed voices. I try not to giggle at my mom's furious expression and lean down, grabbing a glass of champagne as I pass. There's an awkward silence in the room as the people around me struggle to know what to do in the circumstances, so I look around and beam, "Hi everyone, fancy seeing you here."

My mom makes toward me but I turn and walk slap bang into a broad chest, and the familiar scent almost makes me pass out on the spot. Two strong arms catch hold of my arms and as I feel the familiar grip, my legs turn to jelly and all my earlier bravado evaporates in a heartbeat. Time stands still as the past returns to collect its baggage. The world fades away as I am transported back in time to a place where I felt loved and cherished. It was an exciting time, full of hope and enthusiasm that was shattered in a heartbeat one fateful night.

Pulling back, I lift my eyes and stare into the deep velvet pools of my own weakness. "Hello Angelica."

"It's Angel now."

Pulling back, I try to create distance between us, but Sebastian doesn't appear keen to oblige as he keeps me locked in his arms. It feels a little awkward because I can feel the tension in the room as the people in it watch with interest, until a sharp voice cuts in, "Look at the state of you, really Angelica, what happened to you, you look like a…"

"Whore, yes, I've already heard that one, sis, you'll need to be a little more original in your choice of words."

Sebastian's arms fall to his side, and I gasp for air. Anastasia stands by his side looking so furious it makes me giggle and she hisses, "Do you think this is funny? For god's sake, show some respect. You may not be but the rest of us are grieving and this is not the time or place to make it all about you as you usually do."

I stare at her in surprise but before I can even answer my mother says loudly, "Now we're all here, we need to take our seats in Harvey's den." Her voice falters as she brushes an imaginary tear away, and I watch in disbelief as Mr. Featherstone takes her arm and helps her from the room. Anastasia grabs hold of Sebastian's arm and says in a sickly sweet voice, "Come, darling, I'll need your support because this is sure to be extremely upsetting."

Seeing her hand on him, twists the knife once again and I swallow hard. Not daring to look at them, I turn away and follow the small gathering into my father's den and once again the stench of the man himself comes back to bite me. Mr. Featherstone is sitting behind the huge antique desk, and there are various seats set out around the room. My mother's sitting at the front, and she looks around and calls Anastasia forward to take the seat beside her. She half turns toward me, so I quickly take a seat in the furthest corner away from all of them and try to blend into the shadows. I note that Sebastian makes no move to sit beside Anastasia, much to her annoyance, and sits across the room in my direct line of vision. He doesn't shift his eyes from me, and I shrink under the intensity of his dark gaze. Yes, there is unfinished business between us and far from being put off back at the cabin, he obviously appears keen to have his say.

However, that will have to wait because Mr. Featherstone clears his throat and silence takes up residence while we all wait to hear the final will and testament of a monster.

CHAPTER 10

SEBASTIAN

I should never have come. I almost backed out several times over the weekend, but only the thought of seeing her again kept me going. Anastasia was angry that I left the funeral, but I couldn't care less what she thinks. I still can't believe she's still intent on going through with this engagement. It is and always was, a complete sham. As soon as we announced it to the world, my life ended. I had my reasons for agreeing to something I never had any intention of following through, and I paid the highest price for my own principles.

Seeing Angelica today has changed nothing and yet everything. When she stumbled into my arms, a bolt of longing surged through me and I held on tight. She's mine and always has been. I longed to pull her close and lose myself in heaven. She always smelled amazing and still does. Those beautiful blue eyes that I used to drown in looked at me with five years of hurt and betrayal reflected in them. Her bottom lip trembled, and it took all my strength not to take it with mine and taste the perfection that makes all other women seem second best. I saw the fire in her eyes and pictured her astride me, using that passion for a different kind of battle and I wanted to sweep her in my arms and run off into the sunset with her like I should have done all those years ago. Now she's sitting a few feet away and my mind is fucked. I can't concentrate on anything but her and if I'm here for anyone - it's her.

"Excuse me, may I have your attention."

I hear the nervous voice of the attorney and my attention focuses on what he's about to say.

"Thank you for coming and may I begin by extending my sympathies to you all. Harvey Johnson was an impressive man and well respected by all who knew him."

There's a gentle murmur of agreement and one incredibly loud yawn. Trying to stifle my grin, I see Angelica examining her nails with her legs crossed revealing the longest legs I have ever seen and I feel the lust making it uncomfortable to sit still, as the blood rushes to the part of me that has always made me hers. I see the irritable look her mother throws her and Anastasia shakes her head disapprovingly.

"Um… yes, well… shall we begin?"

He looks around for some kind of permission before shuffling some papers on the desk and clearing his throat.

"Ok, there are many parts to this will and the people gathered here stand to inherit some part of his estate. I think it may be best to start with a letter he wrote that sets things out in its most simplistic form and then we can expand on the detail once the news sinks in."

He coughs again and takes a sip of water and then adopts a look of resignation before saying. *"So, it appears that I'm dead."*

Mrs. Johnson sobs and yet the rest of the room is silent.

"Um… anyway, well, *I would have liked to see what freeloaders turned up to hear what I left them but it was not to be. Firstly, I would like to thank my wife for thirty years of boredom."*

There's a collective gasp as all eyes turn to the woman herself and Mr. Featherstone says apologetically, "I'm so sorry, Mrs. Johnson."

"It's fine, just read the letter."

Her voice is tight and bitter and I watch with fascination as the grieving widow mask slips a little. "Um... well, *to my greedy, grasping, bitch of a wife, I leave the house and everything in it. She can continue to sponge off me in death as she did all my life. Her income will come from a percentage of the profits from Johnson plastics, which should keep her in the style to which she has become accustomed to. Then there are my two daughters, Angelica and Anastasia. Two further disappointments that were my cross to bear."*

I look across at Angelica and see the fury in her eyes and feel like sprinting across and wrapping her in my arms to keep the cruel words from hurting her. However, she looks down and I see her digging her nails into her palms as she waits for the rest. Anastasia meanwhile, has started wailing like a banshee which only makes me irritated until her mother says sharply, "Pull yourself together."

Once again, Mr. Featherstone clears his throat and continues. *"I never wanted girls but obviously never had a choice. Two weak minded little dolls who resembled their mother in wanting everything handed to them on a plate. Well, not on my watch girls and so this is what I have for you. Anastasia you get nothing, of worth, anyway. Like your mother your inheritance is directly linked to the company and you will receive a small share of the profits each year. Maybe one day that idiot of a fiancé will actually make an honest woman of you but I can't really blame him for stalling."*

I feel the rage burning up inside as I think of the man who wrote those words. The vile creature who orchestrated my downfall to suit his own agenda and is now labeling me weak for agreeing to it. I make a fist and wish he was still alive so I could end his life myself but I know he has had the last laugh, in this case, anyway. *"And to my absent daughter Angelica, I leave..."* Mr. Featherstone looks up and finds Angelica before saying kindly, "I um... *leave... my company.*"

The room falls silent as all eyes turn in her direction and I see the shock in her eyes as she gasps, "What the fuck?"

"Angelica, language!"

Her mother looks absolutely ruined, but it's nowhere near as shocked as Anastasia looks. "You have got to be kidding me... her... why?"

Angelica sits like a statue as Mr. Featherstone says firmly, "Let me finish. *Yes, that's surprised you, hasn't it? Well, in the absence of actually having someone worth leaving the only thing I really love to, she is the best option. However, Angelica ran out on this family and may not even be listening to this little speech. She has thirty days to claim this inheritance and take her seat on the board, or it falls to her sister. Yes, I'm just glad I'm dead already because the thought of my youngest daughter getting her greedy hands on the family business would kill me all over again.*"

Mr. Featherstone looks up and I can tell he is hating every minute of this as he says softly, "There are many bequests and codicils to the will that I will discuss when you are ready but the bulk of the fortune falls to Angelica."

He looks at her and says gently, "Maybe if you wait behind, we can discuss this in finer detail after the rest is announced. It must be a lot to take in."

I can tell she is struggling and yearn to make everything better for her but she has the look of someone who wouldn't welcome it as she stares at the attorney with a defiant look and says loudly, "No need. If you don't mind, I'll leave you all to hear the rest because I've heard enough. I need some air and so maybe you can forward me the details and I'll study them in private."

She fiddles in her purse and pulls out a business card and

standing up, heads across the room and hands it to the surprised attorney. Then, without even looking at her family, she walks from the room with a straight back and a bravery that makes my heart swell.

Her mom turns back to Mr. Featherstone and says tightly, "Finish it."

As he starts to speak, I slip out of the room. Nobody sees me go and I only have one aim in mind. Find Angelica and check she's ok. The rest can wait because if I know her, her world has just been turned upside down and she won't know what to do about it.

The door slams as I make my way into the hallway and I see Martha looking after her seemingly upset. I don't stop to ask and just head after her and see her racing toward her truck. As she reaches for the door, I place my hand over hers. "Angelica. Stop."

Spinning around, she says angrily, "It's fucking Angel, you idiot. Angelica died when her heart was ripped from her by a man who should have been better. A man she trusted and thought was everything. As it turns out that man was just like all the rest and a total dipshit."

"A dipshit?"

"Yes, a fucking dipshit, and I'm looking at him now."

She puts her hands on her hips and yells, "What I don't understand is why you're out here at all. I mean, the woman you are supposed to be madly in love with is sitting inside probably wondering where her devoted boyfriend is. Instead, you're out here chasing after someone who forgot you five years ago because you are a fucking dipshit who she can't stand the mere mention of."

Despite everything I want to laugh and she knows it because she tosses her hair back and says ominously, "You're a jerk, Sebastian and everyone knows it. Now fuck off back to your bad choice in life and leave me to get on with mine."

"No!"

"No - are you serious?"

"Shut the fuck up, Angel and listen to me, or so help me I'll put you over my knee and spank you out here in broad daylight."

My words have the desired effect because just for a second she is speechless. Then she leans forward and sneers, "I'd like to see you fucking try."

With a quick flick of my wrist, I pull her toward me and then to my surprise she catches me with a move that shows she's learned a thing or two and frees herself and pushes me hard with a force that shows the strength of the woman as she snarls, "How dare you lay your unwelcome hands on me. Don't you ever touch me again because then I will have to kill you."

"Kill me, you're such a drama queen."

"A drama queen, am I? Well, let me tell you, I don't take kindly to men forcing themselves on me so be warned. Keep your distance and I may spare you. Touch me again and I'll break your fucking arm, followed by your legs and finish with your neck, got it?"

I feel the tension between us that she is trying hard to disguise with words and as she catches her breath, I reach out and push her hard against the truck and fisting her hair in my hands, I punish her bold filthy mouth with mine and do what I've been aching to do for five, long torturous years - lose myself and all my principles for just one stolen kiss with the woman I love.

I almost think I've achieved the impossible and reversed time as we share a kiss. Not the first and definitely not the last if I get my way. Then, without any forewarning, I find myself falling to the ground clutching my balls as she delivers a knockout punch that steals the breath from my body. The pain clouds my mind as she breaks away and slams the door on me before reversing off in a hail of gravel, leaving me gasping for air.

By the time the pain subsides she's gone and all that's left is the realization I am ruined forever because despite what happened next, that kiss reinforced everything I've known since she left. I love her and always have and now it's up to me to make things right if I stand a chance of winning her back.

CHAPTER 11

ANGEL

I called him a dipshit. Great, way to go Angel. Of all the things I could have said, I called him a dipshit.

Groaning, I punch the steering wheel and raise my finger at the man who dared sound his horn as I pull out on him. Dipshit. For fuck's sake.

Strangely, that's all I can focus on as I drive, trying to create as much distance as possible between us and my fingers fly to my lips to touch the place where his fell. We kissed. I can't believe we shared a kiss after all these years.

I feel so angry with myself for loving every second of it and hate the weakest part of me that wanted more. Then I despise the woman in me who wasn't content to stop there. I wanted him so badly I could have forgiven him for the pain he inflicted on me just for a few moments of something so intoxicating it makes me an addict desperate for their next fix. Sebastian Stone is my preferred drug of choice and it will kill me in the end. I know that, which is what made me run. I can't let him inside my head, never again. It will finish me off forever, but we *kissed*, and it felt as if I was where I belonged.

The tears start to fall as I feel the loss all over again. How could he have done what he did and choose my sister over me? As betrayals go, it was the ultimate one and now I'm right back where we started because I still want him. Hell, I crave him like the oxygen I need to survive. I close my eyes and see him. I always have and in a moment of weakness I let him inside my head again. Now's who the dipshit?

It's funny how he's the first thing I think of after the knockout punch my father delivered. The air leaves my lungs as the words of his will sink in. The company - he left it to me. Why would he do that? I can't believe it because I don't know the first thing about it. What do I do? Take him up on his kind offer, or let my hated sister take charge and watch our inheritance disappear along with the company inside a year. Should I just let her have it along with *him* while I walk away, leaving them to a happily ever after? It may be for the best because staying would only set me on their path on a daily basis.

My mind shifts back to that kiss and the tears splash onto the steering wheel as I think about what I've lost. We were so happy and so in love, which is why it doesn't make sense. He chose *her*.

Wiping my tears away with the back of my hand, I struggle to make sense of my thoughts. I need to decide quickly though because this is one of those forks in the road that has consequences.

The attorney's words echo around my brain as I think about what they mean. Thirty days to make an important decision and emotion needs to be discarded in favor of hard facts. Can I do this, can I really take charge of a company I know nothing about? Knowing my father, he's left nothing to chance and there is more to this than meets the eye.

I think I must drive around for hours because the day soon turns to night. As I turn onto the dusty track that leads to the cabin, I feel tired, weary, and hungry. Maybe sleep is the answer and when I wake up everything will make sense. I certainly hope so because I don't know what on earth to do next and have nobody to ask? I could make a call and run it through with my new family. Ryder would know what to do, and it's tempting. However, I rely on the Reapers way too much already and I need to prove my self-worth and make this decision based on what I want, not what's the right thing to do. Can I walk away? I already know the answer to that before my head hits the pillow.

∼

Mr. Featherstone is as good as his word and emails the details of daddy's will across and I spend the next few days poring over every paragraph. Luckily, there is enough food in the cabin to keep me going for weeks, so I don't move and just study every word of a bitter and twisted man's last wish. The thing I love the most is that my family will be reliant on the company doing well. It strikes me that if I ran the company into the ground, we would all end up with nothing. It's tempting, so tempting, and I relish the images of mom and Anastasia's faces as I inform them there are no profits to keep them in the lifestyle they love. Hmm, maybe I could demand they actually work for once—for me. Yes, that would be fun. However, even the thought of having contact with them is a punishment not worth contemplating, so my mind runs in circles as I struggle to decide on the right thing to do.

∼

Exactly one week later since the will was read, I make contact with Mr. Featherstone.

The next day we meet and I sign my life away.

Then at 8 am the very next morning, I park my truck in

the parking space that has my father's name on it and walk with purpose toward the revolving door of Johnson's plastics. It's time to start work.

The minute I enter the polished reception of my father's company, I almost turn and head back outside. Any doubts I had resurface and laugh in my face. What was I thinking? I can't do this, I'm no chairman. Hell, I was serving drinks in a bar a few weeks ago and now I'm bold enough to think I can run a company the size of this with no experience. It's a nonsense.

The receptionist looks up with curiosity as I make my way across the polished floor and I know I look the part if nothing else. My tailored suit is fitted, and the skirt falls just above the knee. The crisp white shirt I'm wearing is smart but unbuttoned just enough to preserve my modesty but demonstrate my femininity. My hair hangs long down my back and my makeup provides the mask I hide behind as I say in a strong voice to disguise my nerves, "Good morning, I'm Angel Johnson and have come to take my father's place. Please, can you arrange the necessary security clearance and direct me to his office?"

Her eyes widen and she looks at me in disbelief. I give her a moment to process the information and just stare at her with a hard expression before she stutters, "Um… of course… please accept my condolences, Miss. Johnson for your loss."

I just nod as I watch her trembling fingers punch something on her computer and then she says into her headset, "Excuse me, sir, this is reception. I have a Miss. Johnson here who is… um… here to take Mr. Johnson's place."

She listens and I see the relief in her eyes as she passes the burden onto somebody else and visibly relaxes as she turns to me and says kindly, "Somebody will be down shortly to escort you upstairs."

She pushes a book toward me and says sweetly, "Please can I ask you to sign in until we arrange your ID and security clearance."

I do as she says and then take a seat as I wait for whoever she called. All around me the workers arrive and head for their place of work and I wonder about their lives. What they do, their families - their lives. This company provides the wages that make those lives bearable and I wonder if they are paid well for turning up here every day. As I sit and watch, it heaps a whole load of responsibility onto my shoulders as I feel the burden that's been thrust on them weighing me down. The self-doubts creep in and my breathing comes fast, reminding me I'm way out of my depth. What was I thinking, this isn't a game, people's lives are at stake? Maybe I should just leave and let Anastasia bear this burden, because I'm not sure I can see it through.

"Miss. Johnson?"

Looking up, I see curiosity in the eyes of a smart woman looking at me with a kind expression. She smiles, and it settles my nerves a little as she says kindly, "I'm pleased to meet you. My name's Dora and I am—sorry—was, your father's personal assistant. Please may I extend my most sincere condolences for your loss? He was a…"

"Bastard."

I see the shock in her eyes and almost laugh out loud. Standing up, I smooth down my skirt and smile. "It's ok, Dora, you don't have to pretend around me. We both know what he was like and I must give you credit for sticking this job out, it can't have been easy."

I watch her lips twitch and hold out my hand. "You can call me Angel; I'm pleased to meet you."

She grasps my hand and shakes it warmly and then nods

toward the bank of elevators. "Follow me, and I'll show you to your office. I expect you have many questions and I will try to do my best to answer them."

I follow her and feel my heart settle a little. She seems nice, not what I expected at all. Maybe this won't be so bad. She can fill me in on how things work and as soon as I can, we will start advertising this position because I'm not deluded enough to think I can actually do this. No, as soon as possible, I am hiring someone who can and intend on just setting things up so this company runs itself. Then I'll sit back and watch the profits roll in while I get on with my life—my way. Yes, my mind was made up somewhere in the early hours because this is my big chance and I'm not going to waste it. I will prove my daddy wrong when he said he was disappointed with his family. I am going to do what's right for me and me alone and to hell with the lot of them.

CHAPTER 12

ANGEL

Dora seems pleasant enough. I follow her into the elevator and watch as she presses the button for the top floor. Typical. I'm guessing my father set himself up in his ivory tower, relishing the fact the workers were literally beneath him. As we travel past the many floors, I try to ease the tension that's building, mainly inside me, and say brightly, "How long have you worked here, Dora?"

"Ten years."

"Wow, you deserve a medal."

She laughs softly. "Not really. I started as a junior secretary in the Accounts department and gradually worked my way up."

"Do you like working here?"

"I do as it happens. Mr. Johnson was demanding, but diligent. Mainly I like my co-workers and as jobs go, it's not a bad one."

"Yes, you've summed up my father perfectly, demanding, definitely, and diligent was a word created to describe him. I expect the staff are worried now he's gone. I mean, nobody likes change, right?"

"I suppose so."

She smiles, and it strikes me that she doesn't seem bothered at all. In fact, it must be weird for her talking to somebody who has blown in off the street and made herself in charge. Credit to Dora, nothing appears to faze her.

The elevator reaches its destination, and my heart thumps as I follow her outside. The marble tiled floor indicates that my father liked the finer things and the painted walls are bright and welcoming. We pass various doors and I see brass name plates on them and yet I don't recognize a single one of them. Come to think of it, none of us knew what our father did when he left in the morning. I feel a little excited to find out and discover the man the people inside this building knew far better than his own family.

Finally, we reach his office because the name outside reveals it. Dora stops and smiles and to my surprise, raises her hand to knock. She looks almost apologetic as a deep voice shouts, "Come in."

As she pushes the door open, my jaw hits the floor because sitting behind my father's desk, looking so cocky it makes my heart bleed, is Sebastian Stone.

I barely hear the words they exchange before Dora leaves, closing the door softly behind her. All I can think of is the pain twisting inside me as I see the cocky son of a bitch staring at me, looking so hot I almost want to rip my clothes off and demand he takes me right here on that desk. However, that would be over my dead body because I would rather kill myself than allow him near me after what he did, so instead, I use words to hide behind and snarl, "You're in my seat."

He sits back and appraises me, which irritates the hell out of me as he looks me up and down. I feel stripped bare by that look as he rakes me from head to toe and leaves me panting inside. He always was good-looking, but the last five years have developed him into some kind of Adonis. His sharp suit hangs well on him and the white shirt unbuttoned just enough to reveal a tantalizing glimpse of hard flesh makes my knees weak. The stubble sits well on his face and his dark eyes flash as he shoots me a look loaded with so much desire it takes my breath away. Then he smiles, but it has no humor in it and says in a deep voice, "Sit."

He gestures to the seat in front of the desk and I snarl, "I'm not a dog for you to command. How dare you sit in my chair and issue me orders as if you're in charge? Now get out and don't come back."

"Sit!"

I stare at him incredulously and his eyes twinkle, making me so mad I could rip my stiletto off and embed it in his skull from across the room. Taking a few deep calming breaths, I say in a low controlled voice, "I asked you nicely and still you sit there issuing your orders like the complete idiot you are. Now, I will ask you again and this time you will do as I say because You. Are. Sitting. In. My. Seat. Please leave."

To my surprise, he does as I ask and stands. As he ventures out from behind the desk, I swallow hard. Without breaking eye contact, he prowls toward me and my legs start shaking at the power in his stare and as he reaches me, I almost close my eyes and offer my lips to his willingly before he takes hold of my arm and propels me toward the chair. Then he forces me into the seat and holds me in place, saying firmly, "I said *sit* you infuriating woman and listen because god help me, if you challenge me again, I will put you over my knee and take great pleasure in spanking that fine ass of yours until you can't sit down for a week."

I open my mouth to tell him exactly what I think about that, but before I can his mouth covers mine and his tongue ties mine in knots as he kisses me so hard and so deep, I forget even my own name. Despite everything that's happened between us, I kiss him back. I can't help it because he makes me weak. He makes me forget all the strength I stored up in anger over the past five years and makes me forget everything but him. I feel so disappointed in myself because I can't deal with the emotion he puts me through. I am just not strong enough to win this war because he still owns my heart, and I have to figure out a way to snatch it right back before I can possibly win against him.

The cold air rushes between us, fanning the flames as he pulls back and retreats behind my desk. Taking his seat, he stares at me with a look so hot I get an immediate tan as I stare at him in shock. "Now I have your attention we will begin."

I say nothing because I don't have words. I don't have anything because he has beaten me and he knows it. I see the arrogance of a man who always liked to be in control and if nothing, it has just intensified over the past five years and so I let him speak—at last.

"It's good to see you, Angel."

I shrug, and it annoys me to see the amusement in his eyes as he leans back. "Congratulations on your inheritance, it must have come as quite a shock."

Still, I say nothing and he shakes his head. "Fine. Enough of the pleasantries, it's time you learned the facts. You inherited your father's company which actually amounts to a share of 55% of it."

I try not to let him see the shock his words bring and just focus on the picture of my hated father on the wall behind him. "My father was Harvey's partner and in fact, set up the company alongside him all those years ago. However, circumstances meant that his share dwindled over the years and now our family own 25%. The other 20% was sold to various shareholders over time to raise much needed capital."

The bitterness in his voice makes me look up and the look in his eye tells me this isn't some cozy little tale he's about to tell.

"You see, Angel, my father was a very weak man. He may have been good at his job, but he, as it turns out, wasn't good at life. Where your father relished the cut throat nature of the business, mine did not. He preferred to adopt a more passive role in the company and allowed your father to deal with the unsavory details of building an empire."

I almost pity him and say softly, "I'm sorry, I never knew; he always seemed so competent."

Sebastian's eyes flash. "He was. Competent, I mean, but he lacked the killer instinct your father had. The reason his share value dwindled was because he gambled it away. He kept it a secret from everyone, even your father and the shares he sold weren't sold through the usual channels."

This conversation is unexpected and despite my anger toward him, I feel sorry for the man before me. He looks destroyed and I can tell he is hating every moment of his little speech.

"Your father discovered that a local mobster now owned a fifth of his company. My father had gambled it away over time, and he was happy to allow him. You see, Tobias Moretti is the type of man who scars men, both physically and mentally. He recognized the weakness in my father and exploited it."

Interrupting, I say quickly, "So, you're saying we have to do business with a… criminal?"

Nodding, Sebastian sighs heavily. "It appears so. You see, there are three of us in this partnership, you, me and Tobias."

He must see the fear in my eyes because he says in a softer voice, "However, Tobias is not interested in heading up a company. He is more interested in running a crime family. He has mainly left the business of managing Johnson's plastics to our fathers and is just keen to receive the dividends his share brings. The trouble is, now your father's um…"

"Dead."

"Yes - dead, he may not be so trusting. I'm sure that when he hears the terms of your father's will, he'll be demanding a meeting and we may not like what we hear."

Shrugging, I cross my legs and lean forward. "I'm not afraid of him."

Sebastian looks angry. "For fuck's sake, Angelica, this isn't a game. Don't you see we are in a bad situation here and I don't think you realize how serious it is. You have no experience of running this company and are vulnerable. You don't stand a chance against a man like Tobias and neither do I."

"What about you, Sebastian, what has any of this got to do with you, anyway? Your father owns a quarter of this company, not you, so, where is he? Why isn't he sitting in my daddy's chair and taking charge because surely he's the best man for the job?"

"He's dead."

I see the pain in Sebastian's eyes, and it hits me hard. My first instinct is to run and comfort him because I know how much Sebastian loved his father. Where I hated mine, he adored his and I know how devastated he must be.

I make to move toward him, but he holds up his hand. "Don't bother, I don't need your pity."

His words surprise me and he laughs bitterly. "It's been four years now; I can cope with it; I don't need anyone to hold my hand and tell me everything will be ok."

He turns away and looks out at the city that lies beneath us and says in a dull voice.

"Whatever you think of me doesn't matter now. You have

a decision to make and you had better think with your head rather than your conflicted heart."

"What decision?"

My words sound cold and hollow even to my ears as I recognize something's changed since I walked inside this office. "Sign your share over to your sister and walk away back to the new life you made and keep yourself safe."

"Or?"

He spins around, and I almost gasp as I see the pure torture in his eyes. "Or stay and fight but know this battle may be one you lose."

"What battle, you forget I'm the majority shareholder. He can't touch me?"

"Keep telling yourself that, Angelica, because you're not strong enough to play with the big, bad, boys, no matter how much you think you are."

His words irritate the hell out of me and I stand, feeling so angry I can't breathe. Thumping my fist on the desk he sits behind, daring to try to chase me out of town. I snarl, "I don't care what you think, Sebastian. You may think your stupid story will chase me away, but it won't. You obviously have an extremely low opinion of me, well, right back at you. You know, you would love nothing more for me to spin on my heels and leave you to your happy ever after with my sister. I get it now. You'll marry my hated sister and gain control of the company. She is weak and willing and would be only too happy to let you take charge, while she sits in the mansion you provide and plays dress up. I'm not stupid and this is all probably just a horror story you've made up to scare me off. Well, fuck you because this is now my company and you are sitting in my seat!"

Just for a moment, we lock eyes in a battle of wills. He is furious. I can see that and I feel a sense of victory as he realizes there is nothing he can do about the situation we are now in. Shaking his head angrily, he thumps the desk and yells, "For fuck's sake, Angelica, open your eyes and do the right thing. Back off and let me deal with this."

"It's Angel now, you complete and utter butt head. Why can't you grasp such a basic fact. Now, as I said, you're sitting at my desk and if you don't mind, I want to start work. So, run along and do what someone who is second in command does with his day because I'm in charge now and things are about to change."

To my surprise, Sebastian stands and moves away from the desk, saying roughly, "Fine, have it your way - *Angel*." His tone is sarcastic as he says my name. "Have it your way but I give you until the end of the day before you come begging me to come back and help you out of the hole you've just jumped into head first. Do it your way and this company will destroy itself in less than a week. Then we'll all have nothing."

As he makes to leave, I say angrily, "Maybe that's my plan all along."

He turns and I say bitterly, "You see, Sebastian, you think I want this business to survive. You think I want to make a go of it and provide a comfortable living for my family. Well, newsflash, I don't. You see, I owe you all nothing. If I owe anyone anything, it's me, Angel. No, my decision was based on one thing only - closure. If Tobias whatshisname wants to buy me out, then the only consideration is the price. Then I can take his tainted money and break any ties I have with you all forever. No, my shares are for sale and I don't care who buys them. So, run along and stew on that because as far as I'm concerned there is no fight left in me - I don't care anymore."

The door slamming is all the answer I get and I sink down onto the seat opposite the one my father used to own. As I stare at his hated pompous face staring at me from the painting on the wall, I smirk at it. "Revenge is sweet, daddy dearest, and I bet you never saw this one coming. How does it feel knowing your beloved company that you worked so hard to build, is about to be torn down by the disappointment you trusted it to? Rest in peace you miserable bastard because I'm about to walk away from the lot of you."

CHAPTER 13

SEBASTIAN

I am furious. So furious I need to get the hell out of here before I do something I'll regret. I'm not sure what happened to her over the last five years but she's returned a very different person than the one who left.

Dora looks at me with concern as I pass, but I don't say anything. I can't even speak because suddenly shits got real—for all of us. I never thought Angelica would be so bitter and twisted as to jeopardize everything in this flippant way. She obviously doesn't have a clue about what's at stake and I should make every effort to enlighten her, but I can't. It hurts so much to look at her with the pain in her eyes reflected back at me, knowing I'm the person responsible for putting it there.

As I slam the door to my office shut, I pace the floor and wrestle with my guilty conscience. I had to do what I did - for my father. It was Hobson's choice, and I did what was best at the time.

Moving across to the panoramic window, I look down on the city below. How I envy the people that walk the streets. I hope they are happy because nobody deserves to feel the pain I've lived with ever since that day and now I don't have a clue how to dig myself out of the huge hole I'm in.

There's a gentle tap at the door and I shout, "I don't want to be disturbed."

It annoys me even further when the door opens slowly and my assistant's voice says shakily, "Um… sorry, sir, but your fiancée's here and is demanding to see you."

I feel the irritation crawl over me as I snap, "Fine, send her in."

Great, just what I need.

The door opens and Anastasia sweeps into the room, dressed completely in black, looking like the black widow. Her face is pale, and she has perfected the look of a woman shrouded in grief. However, I know it's just a show and feel irritated that she's even here, so I snap, "I don't have time for this."

I don't miss the hurt flare in her eyes, and yet I don't care. In my mind she's the huge wedge between me and the woman I love and I've run out of patience with this whole sorry charade.

"Someone's tetchy this morning."

Her voice is laced with derision and I say wearily, "What do you want, Anastasia?"

She flings her purse onto the desk and unwraps her coat, letting it fall from her shoulder. As it drops to the ground, I blink in disbelief as she stands before me in sheer black underwear, with stockings and suspenders. She licks her lips and stands suggestively before me and says in a low voice, "I won't wait anymore, Sebastian. We're engaged to be married and yet you won't come close. I've been patient for five long years because you told me you didn't believe in sex before marriage. Why would you tell me such an obvious lie unless it was because you respect me too much to taint the goods before the big day?"

I stare at her in disbelief as she purrs, "I mean, I know you're a gentleman, but a lady has needs. Well, I'm here to tell you there's no need to be the gentleman. I want you and as it happens, I don't want to wait anymore. Daddy's dead so you don't have to fear pistols at dawn. I'm willing and... well, you've been patient for far too long, so what's stopping us?"

I take a step back because I didn't expect this. It's true I have kept her at arm's length for the past five years and not because of the reasons she thinks. I can't stand her and never have done. The thought of touching her makes my skin crawl, and she's so wrapped up in her own importance she can't see that. We have never even kissed, which makes me wonder why she keeps on playing this obvious game of charades. I act as her partner on social occasions and play the part of the perfect fiancé in public, but keep the hell away from her in private. Is she really that obtuse to think we have a relationship?

Shaking my head, I say as gently as possible, "Put the coat back on, Anastasia, this isn't going to happen."

Her eyes flash and she advances toward me, swaying her hips and pouting suggestively as she drawls, "Now, come on, honey, I've heard the rumors."

"What rumors?"

"The ones that whisper you're not averse to the kinky stuff. I mean, it's common knowledge you like to spend your time at a certain, um... club in town. I know you go there to satisfy your carnal urges, and that's fine by me. I know a man has... needs and so do I. I'm here to tell you it's ok to act on them because I'm here and willing to satisfy yours. We don't have to wait until we're married, you know. I'm not the princess you think I am."

I stare at her open mouthed as she reaches me and runs her fingers through my hair, pressing her almost naked body to mine and whispering, "Kiss me, Sebastian. I know you've been longing to. Well, this is your chance. I want you and what better time than this. We will be a proper couple and I'm not afraid who knows. It's time to move our relationship on, so kiss me my darling and don't hold back."

She presses her lips to mine and as I feel her soft lips go where they are most unwelcome, I pull back sharply and say roughly, "No."

"NO!" I see the fury in her eyes as I say harshly, "It's not gonna happen, so get your coat on and leave before I say something both of us will regret."

I see the panic enter her eyes as she whispers, "Please, Sebastian, I need you. I just want us to be a proper couple. This isn't right. This distance between us, I need more, I can handle it, I'm not the innocent virgin you think I am."

Her hand flies to her mouth as if to contain the words she just said, and I laugh. "Not a virgin. I wonder what your dear daddy would make of that."

She steps back and says quickly, "It was only the once, years before we met, of course, I don't sleep around, I would never do that to you."

I feel the exasperation bubbling up inside, along with a sudden feeling of pity. This isn't right, it never was and so I say a little kindlier, "Put your coat back on and take a seat."

Noting the softer tone to my voice, she moves away and retrieves her coat before wrapping it around her. Then she takes a seat on the couch in my office and I sit beside her and say softly, "We both know this isn't normal, don't we?"

Her eyes widen and she says fearfully, "I'm sorry, Sebastian, I should never have come here like this. I just wanted… you."

The tears splash onto her cheeks and I feel like a complete and utter bastard as I say something I should have said from the beginning. "The engagement is off, Anastasia, it should never have been on in the first place."

For a moment she stares at me in disbelief and then her voice quivers. "Why?"

I can't believe she's even asking, but now I need to spell it out for her no matter how cruel my words sound. "Because your daddy made it impossible for me not to agree to it."

"Daddy?"

"Yes, I only agreed to marry you because he gave me no other choice. Now he's gone, I need to set you free to find a man who will love you as you always deserved to be loved."

Shaking her head, she says slowly, "But I thought..."

"That this was real? I never once gave you that impression. If anything, I hoped that my distance would make you call it off, but you never did. Why is that, why did you go ahead with something that was so wrong from the start?"

Her lips tremble and she says with a break in her voice, "Because I wanted you, Sebastian, not anyone else. It was always you."

"But why, I never gave you any cause to think I was interested. Why me?"

I see the shock wearing off as her eyes flash and she says bitterly, "Because you are the best. The best looking and the one all the girls want. You always were. They all wanted you; surely you knew that. No other guy could compare and I want the best in life and that was you. But you never saw me. You only saw one girl—her. Is this what this is, Angelica's back and now you want to clear the way for getting back with her?"

I look down and she snarls, "I figured as much. You know, you may be some smart assed businessman now, Sebastian, but you're still that kid who followed her around like a puppy dog. Well, let me tell you, she's not interested. Why do you think she left and never came back? Because she doesn't care. Knowing my sister, she's not been as devoted in her time away. I'm guessing there have been many men and none of them you. So, get over it and move on with someone who deserves your attention because that cold bitch will leave you as soon as she's finished playing the big shot and won't look back."

Her voice changes and she says softly, "Give her up and marry me, Sebastian, I'll make you happy; happier than she ever will."

Standing up, I cross the room to get some distance between us and just say sharply, "Get out and consider this engagement terminated. I'll post an announcement in the press and say it was you who ended it if that makes you feel any better."

I feel her fury from here as she snarls, "I won't let you make a fool of me, no, Sebastian, this marriage stands and you will go through with it, because if you don't, as soon as this company is mine, I will make it my life's work to destroy you and leave you with nothing."

She stands and smoothes down her coat before saying in a hard voice, "It's your choice, darling. Marry me and have it all, or pine after my sister and lose everything. You have until tomorrow to make your decision. Then we will get this wedding moving and begin our married life together. I know you'll make the right decision, you're too smart to risk everything your daddy worked for. Don't disappoint him, darling, you know this is for the best, it always was."

I say nothing as she leaves my office, just grateful she's gone. Catching sight of the photograph that sits proudly on my desk, I feel my chest tighten as I see the only picture I have of my father with me. I did this all for him and it still wasn't enough. Maybe I should just walk away, it's tempting because suddenly, all the fight in me has gone. Not because of Anastasia. No, it's because the thought of Angelica never wanting me is too much to face. It would break the one remaining part of my heart that still has hope and I would never recover.

CHAPTER 14

ANGEL

As soon as Sebastian left, I sighed with relief. I never expected that—him. Seeing him here in my father's office threw me. Then when he kissed me, I forgot every bad thing that happened and lost myself in my own desire. Now he's gone, I'm back to reality with a bump and as I take my seat of power, I realize just what a hole I've jumped into.

Daddy's desk is clear and well organized. The polished wood reflects my own miserable face and the only personal items on the desk are his ink pen that he used and a photograph of his family when we were young. As I look at the silver-framed picture of a lie, I feel huge regret for something I never really had - a loving family.

We were just like everything around me—his possessions. As we stare at the camera, I remember the day this was taken. Every year we lined up for the official family photograph to mark the passing of time. I must have been seventeen when this one was taken. Even then I knew my life was built on liquid mud. It was difficult to keep a balance in an ever-changing landscape. Daddy's moods were legendary, and both my sister and I were often on the receiving end of his acid tongue.

As I stare at my sister, I feel my blood boil. We never got along, which is no surprise because we are poles apart. She's just like my mother, shallow, vindictive, and vain. All they care about are appearances and looking good among their friends. Content with reaping the rewards of the profits from this company and spending them without a care. Anastasia always ran with the coolest crowd and demanded the most. She wanted the biggest parties and the best of everything. I did not. I just wanted *him* and for many years I had just that. We were happy, or so I thought, until he turned out to be just like the rest of them and drove a jagged dagger into my heart that he never retrieved. Now I am left a broken woman as I battle to re-build the pieces of my shattered dreams.

My gaze lingers on my father, and I feel something like remorse kicking in. I never knew him—not really. He scared me and yet as I see his face staring out of the picture, something hits me about the look in his eyes. He looks lost and kind of sad and for once it strikes me that I never got to know the man behind the overbearing personality. Are we alike? Anastasia is the spitting image of my mom in looks and personality. Maybe I'm more like my father than I thought, which is why he entrusted his life's work to me. Am I as ruthless as him? Am I up to this job and can I really rise to the challenge because he obviously thinks I can?

For the first time since I returned, I think differently.

A tentative knock on the door brings me back to the present and Dora heads in, looking worried. "I'm sorry to intrude, Miss. Johnson, but I wondered if you would like me to fetch you anything. A coffee, some refreshments, information? You name it, I'm here to oblige."

I feel bad as she looks at me hopefully and I say warmly. "Come in Dora and take a seat."

Once she is settled, I smile. "Listen, this is all new to me and I've never had staff before, let alone as many as this. I'll need your support over the next few months and any help would be greatly appreciated. First though, tell me, are you married?"

She looks surprised. "No, unless you count my job, some say I'm married to that."

Her answer surprises me, and I see a gentle flush break out across her face as I study her. Changing tack, I shrug. "It's overrated, if you ask me. I'm in agreement, a job will never break your heart, unlike a man."

She nods, and I see the concern in her eyes as I laugh softly. "Once bitten, twice shy as they say, so we are on the same page. Maybe we will both stay married to this job and see if we can survive in a man's world. Anyway, in answer to your question, a coffee would be good but I'll make it."

She makes to object and I hold up my hand. "Point me in the right direction and while I'm gone, can you please gather together all the staff files for starters? I want to know who works here and get a picture of the people behind the company before I take a look at that company itself. I want names, job descriptions and how long they've been here. I want your honest opinion on the people who work here and then, when we're done, I want you to call a staff meeting."

Standing up, I head toward the door and say brightly, "Right, where's the kitchen?"

"Um… two doors down to your right. There's a small kitchen that we use to make the drinks on this floor. Every floor has one."

"Great, one last question. How do you take yours?"

"Mine?"

"Your coffee."

She looks a little uncomfortable and I'm guessing my father never made one for her and she says softly, "Black, no sugar."

Nodding, I head outside and take a deep breath. I can do this. If I'm about to tear down this company then I need to know what I'm destroying in the process.

It doesn't take long to find the kitchen and I smile as I see everything is clean and tidy. It appears that the staff are conscientious and I'm pleased to see the cupboard is well stocked and there are even some biscuits.

Grabbing a packet, I make the coffees and head outside. However, almost as soon as I'm one foot out the door, I almost drop the mugs I'm carrying when I run into the last person I expected to see—Anastasia.

"What the hell are you doing here?"

She laughs and points to the mugs I'm carrying. "Interesting. It would appear old habits die hard and you can't stop being the good little waitress you are. What's the matter sis, out of your depth and returning to the only thing you're good at."

"At least I'm good at something. Let me see, what exactly are you good at, dear sister, I never did find out?"

She smirks and, to my horror, unfastens her coat revealing some kind of whore's dream wardrobe and she laughs softly, "Looking after my man. You know, Sebastian thinks I'm very good at something as it happens, pleasing him. Yes, he relies on my visits to keep him going through the tedious grind this job brings. So, you see my dearest Angelica, while you were away the cat very much played and found a much more exciting proposition in me."

Once again, the pain slices my heart into little pieces, but I don't give her the satisfaction of seeing it. Instead, I laugh softly. "Goodness, this gives a whole new meaning to a quickie. He only left my office less than half an hour ago.

Either he's lacking stamina, or you're just not good enough to keep him interested. Anyway, some of us have actual work to do so you can see yourself out."

I walk past her and then add, "Oh, and just so you know, for future reference, you are not welcome here. If I see you, I'll have you thrown out. Maybe that will be my first instruction to my staff, keep the trash outside on the sidewalk and don't let it blow inside. You know, Anastasia, you always were easily pleased."

As I walk down the corridor, she screams, "Why did you come back, Angelica, nobody wants you here? Go back to wherever you've been and leave the rest of us to live happily ever after. I give you one week before you fall on that fat ass of yours and make yourself look like a fool."

"Keep telling yourself that, sister, from where I'm standing, the only fool around here is the woman dressed as a cheap whore looking for tricks. Maybe I should call the cops and have you arrested for soliciting. I'm sure that would look good on the front of the society pages."

Slamming the office door behind me, I try to stop myself from crumbling. Images of her and Sebastian together destroy me all over again and as Dora looks up, I hand her the coffee and say tightly, "Please tell security I don't want any of my family allowed access to this building. I also need a moment alone, so, please would it be possible to finish your work at your desk?"

To her credit, Dora just nods. "Of course, consider it done."

She heads outside with her coffee and I'm grateful for her professionalism because I need to be alone with my miserable thoughts as I try to work out if I'm strong enough for this.

Sitting down, I take a huge swig of my coffee and reach

for the phone. As I dial the number I know by heart, I feel my heart settle. I should have done this right from the start.

"Yes."

"It's Angel."

There's a light pause and then in a gentler tone, he says, "Hey, baby, we're worried about you."

I almost crumble but he would not appreciate that, so I ram some steel in my heart to keep it upright and banish all emotion as I've trained myself to do before saying, "I need some help."

"Just ask and it's yours."

"I need information on Tobias Moretti."

"Is he threatening you?"

I hear the ominous tone and smile to myself. Yes, I knew I could count on my family. "Not yet, which is why I need to be armed with information before he does."

"You'll have it within the hour."

My voice almost breaks as the tears threaten to blind me and I hold it together just a fraction of a second longer as I say, "Thanks, Ryder."

I cut the call and lie face down on the desk and cry harder than I have for some time. It's all too much. I knew it would be hard, but this is like a pit of salt waiting beside an open wound. Every step I take, someone throws some in and it burns.

CHAPTER 15

ANGEL

Dora feeds me the information I requested, and I read every word. It appears that daddy had a loyal workforce because they appear to like working here and stay for years. The turnover is small and I can see why. They have good working conditions, higher than average pay and generous holiday entitlement. The healthcare package is a good one and they enjoy many benefits that don't come as standard. My father has surprised me. He obviously valued his staff and treated them right, I'm glad of that at least. Once again, I feel a pang as I think about what I'm planning. Would I really sell out to a criminal just for petty revenge? I'm not so sure anymore and when the information I requested makes its way over to me, I study it with interest.

Sebastian was right to be worried because Tobias Moretti is a felony on legs. He has his fingers in several pies dotted around the city and most of them illegal. I can only wonder why he hasn't been taken out already and wonder if he's the devil that can be controlled.

However, I know enough about men like him to know he won't be a pushover, so I need to up my game before we meet. I can't back down and I need to be firm about what I want because one sign of weakness is all it would take to give him the information he needs to break me all over again.

∼

THE DAY PASSES, and I stay locked in my office. Dora keeps me supplied with food, drink and information and my eyes close long before my resolve and as I see her weary face looking at me, I feel bad. "It's way past clocking off time, Dora, why don't you head home and make sure to come in at lunchtime tomorrow? You've worked hard and I need you fit and well to help me through this."

She looks surprised. "No, I'll be in at 7 am sharp, as always."

Shaking my head, I adopt a fiercer tone. "I insist, bosses orders. Now go and salvage at least some of your evening."

She nods and then says softly, "Will you be ok, Miss. Johnson?"

"It's Angel and yes, I think I will be. Thanks for your help today, I think we'll work well together."

She smiles and heads outside and I know how lucky I am to have her. My gaze falls to my father's photograph and for once I don't have any anger toward him. If anything, I feel a new found respect for the man who obviously valued his employees and I can see why. Here everybody worked well and got the job done. They put in the hours and he reaped the rewards. When he went home, his family grasped what he gave them and never helped in any way. I wonder about the man whose heart gave out in the end. Will I discover that I formed the wrong opinion of him without getting to know him properly first?

Sighing, I decide to head back to the cabin. A few hours'

sleep will help because tomorrow, I intend on facing the staff and I'm still not sure what I'll tell them.

As I close my office door behind me, I notice a light on under a door a few doors away. Feeling curious, I push it open and swallow hard as I see Sebastian poring over his computer screen with only the desk lamp as a companion. He looks weary and defeated and I feel solely responsible for that. He has discarded his jacket and his shirt is unbuttoned showing the smattering of dark hair that I remember well. His stubble filled jaw makes my legs weak with desire and as he raises his weary eyes to mine, I see them darken as he shoots me the usual lust-filled look we always shared.

"Angel."

I nod, noting he used my new name and I thank him for it. A small victory but one that matters—to me, anyway.

"You're working late, what's the matter, did my sister wear you out earlier and you feel you should make up the time?"

"What are you talking about?"

"Anastasia, she was here earlier for your regular booty call I believe."

The anger in his eyes surprises me as he says tightly, "There was and never has been any booty call. You seem to have a very low opinion of me based on your own hurt and anger."

"Can you blame me?"

The look in his eyes shocks me as he fixes me with a pained expression. "No, I don't blame you. I'm sure if I were in your position, I'd feel exactly the same."

I feel curious and against my better judgment, move inside his office and say tentatively, "Maybe now is the time."

"For what?"

He looks guarded and I feel a little anxious as I take the

seat opposite him. "For explanations. You owe me that at least."

Suddenly, I have his full attention and as I feel the full force of it, I swallow hard. When Sebastian looks at me, he sees inside my soul. He always has. He sees things nobody else does and as he stares at me now, I see the understanding in his eyes and he visibly relaxes. A gentle look crosses his face and I push away my desire to head across and curl up on his lap like I used to. He always did offer me comfort when I needed it most and there were many nights that we just sat while he stroked my hair and whispered that he would always look after me.

I can tell he has the same memory because I see the pain in his expression as he says softly, "It was never my intention to marry Anastasia."

"But…"

He holds up his hand and says firmly, "Let me finish."

I fall silent and he sighs wearily. "Your father knew it was you. It always was, but he wasn't happy about that for some reason."

"Why?"

"I never did find out but the day before you left, he called my father and me to his office. Once again, my father had gambled away further shares of the company and to say your daddy was pissed was putting it mildly. You see, Angel, despite what we thought of your father, he lived for this company. He was fearful for its future. Not only was he unwillingly going into business with a criminal but the world was rebelling against the use of plastic. He was fighting on every level and my father was a weak link in the chain that had to be ended."

Sebastian looks so broken my first instinct is to comfort him - but I can't. Whatever his reasons were he betrayed me and I need to hear him out before I can decide if he deserves forgiveness or not.

"As it happens, my father was ill. Terminally."

He raises his eyes to mine and I see the pain intensified in his. "He needed expensive medical care and his healthcare wasn't up to the job. He offered the rest of his shares to your father in return for the treatment but…"

He breaks off and I hold my breath as I picture the scene. Surely daddy helped, he must have done. I almost can't bear to hear the answer because Sebastian looks destroyed.

"He told my father that he only wanted one thing in return. Me."

I feel confused and Sebastian laughs bitterly. "I still remember the hard look in his eye as I sat beside my father. He told me he knew of our relationship and wasn't happy about it. I had dishonored him by taking the innocence of his beloved daughter—his exact words and now I would pay the price. I was to agree to marry Anastasia, to get her off his back as he put it and break all connections with you. He wanted more for you apparently and a relationship with me wasn't in his life plan."

"But why?"

I can't believe what I'm hearing and he says angrily, "Because he didn't think I was good enough. He told me my father's weakness was evidence of that. He wanted somebody strong for you because you were the only hope he had left. You were his heir apparent and needed to be strong and not distracted by love."

The tears fall freely down my face as I whisper, "He wanted me to suffer, to lose the one thing I loved for this… the company's future?"

Sebastian shrugs and says gently, "Probably, yes. Whatever his reasons, he was very clear he didn't want me in your life. Maybe it was a punishment for going behind his back, or maybe he just didn't think I was good enough for you but it appears he wanted to break you to rebuild you a stronger person. Chaining me to Anastasia was the weapon he needed and my biggest regret is that I agreed."

I feel so bitter I almost can't speak. "You gave up on… us."

Sebastian says angrily, "I never gave up on us, I bought us time."

"Time, are you kidding me? You thought by agreeing to marry my sister made you look stronger and would make my daddy accept you. You're a fool, Sebastian. He was testing you. He wanted to see how strong and how committed you really were. Well, as it happens, you failed at the first test, so well done, honey, you get the prize for being the biggest dumb fuck of the lot."

Sebastian brings his fist down on the table and shouts, "I was given no other choice. Agree to marry Anastasia and give my father the treatment he needed to make his last days comfortable. It was an impossible choice. The two most important people in the world to me were being used against me. I had to agree because despite his weaknesses I loved my father and would make the same choice all over again."

I can't help the tears that fall and pull away as Sebastian moves across and kneels before me. He takes my hands in his and says in a broken voice, "I agreed to marry your sister for *him*. When I made that decision, I vowed that was all it would be—a pretense. I never once kissed her, I certainly never touched her, and I just played the fiancé in public. In private I kept my distance and her coming here today was to threaten me all over again."

"What do you mean?"

"She told me that unless we married and become a proper couple, when you leave and she inherits the company, she would make sure I lost everything. She told me it was certain you will leave and I would end up with nothing."

"What did you do?" My voice comes out in a whisper, almost fearful for his answer, as he says firmly, "I broke off our fake engagement and told her to leave."

Reaching up, he strokes the side of my face and says huskily, "It was always you, Angel. You know that. Losing everything was a price I was willing to pay because without you, I have nothing. I did what I had to for my father but now I owe nobody. It's time I did what my heart always wanted and try to win you back. I never wanted to lose you in the first place but you ran before I had the chance to explain. I never stopped loving you and you were always the first thing I thought about when I woke and the last thing at night."

I almost can't breathe as the past swirls around like a choking fog. It seeps into my mind and distorts my feelings. On the one hand, I want to forgive Sebastian and recover a future that was always meant to be, but I have lived with the hurt for five long painful years and I'm not sure it's so easy.

Pulling back, my voice sounds strangled as I say, "I need time."

I don't miss the disappointment in his eyes as he drops my hands and stands up. "Of course, I'll wait for as long as it takes."

Unsure about what to do next, I stand on shaking limbs and clear my throat. "Um… I need to get some rest and think about everything. Maybe you should too."

I turn to leave and his hand on my shoulder causes my heart to beat frantically as he says softly, "Please believe me, Angel. I was never going to marry Anastasia. I did what I had to for my father; I can't change it and would do it again. My biggest regret was that you never got to hear it from me."

It's tempting. So tempting to give into what I know is inevitable but something is preventing me from doing it. It's too much and will take a lot more than words to rebuild the broken person I became, so I just nod. "I believe you, Seb, I'm sorry, I just need time, a lot has happened in the past five years and I'm not the girl who left all those years ago. I'm not sure Angel is who you think she is and you may not like what I've become. Please, let's just deal with the future of this company and worry about the rest another day."

I walk away from Sebastian as is becoming the habit. I walk from the building and wonder about its future.

As I head back to the cabin, I do so with fear in my heart because I'm not sure I am strong enough for the days ahead. My daddy broke me for a reason and now I just need to discover what that reason is.

CHAPTER 16

SEBASTIAN

I'm not sure I slept a wink all night. Angel is so far inside my head, there's no room for me anymore. Every time I see her, I just want to rewind time and make it all better. Five years is a long time to regret one decision. I have been lonely for the entire time because the only physical contact I've had is with the subs at the club. They ask no questions and demand nothing. It's just sex, and I was a fool for thinking it would drive the memory of her away. It didn't. All it did was reinforced the fact I miss her so much my heart hurts more each day. Now she's back and there's so much I want to say and yet my words sound weak and pathetic even to my own ears. No, Angel deserves a strong man, one who will never let her down, so whatever it takes I will stand by her side and see this through—wherever it may lead.

As soon as I step foot inside the office, I know she's here already. Her door is closed, but I know she's inside. We always did have a sixth sense where the other was concerned and I wonder how she's feeling. A staff meeting was called for 9 am today in the boardroom and I sense the unease in the air as the staff fear the worst. I fear nothing except that she will leave. Turn her back on the lot of us and head right back to where she came from.

Thinking of the company she's been keeping makes my blood boil. Bikers. It doesn't bear thinking about and thinking of Angel in their world, being used like a cheap whore is enough to send me over the edge. I try not to think about it but seeing that beast waiting for her that day has painted a picture I'm not keen to dwell on. I did that. I sent her to hell and I have no right to judge her for it.

Pamela, my assistant, smiles as I head toward my office. "Good morning, sir."

I note the tense set to her lips and the worry in her eyes. She is worried about her job, it's obvious but I have no words of comfort. I don't know which way this will go as much as the rest of them and can only hope that Angel has seen enough to make the right decision and not act out of revenge.

For the next hour, I catch up on emails and wonder what's going on inside her head. I wish I knew because it's agony waiting for her to determine all our fate. I only want one thing—her, and if it takes me the rest of my miserable life, I'm going to make it up to her.

"Um... excuse me, Mr. Stone."

Looking up, I see Pamela waiting nervously by the open door. "What is it?"

"Um... Dora told me to add a meeting in the diary for this afternoon and I wanted to check it was ok with you first."

"What meeting?"

"Um... it's at 2 o'clock with Tobias Moretti."

I just nod because I expected this. Angel means business, and it's what I would have done in her shoes.

"Fine, add it to my schedule."

She nods and heads back to her desk, and I wonder what Angel will make of Tobias. I've had the displeasure of meeting him three times and hated every minute of it. He's cold, calculating and cruel, and the thought of sitting across the table from him is not a pleasant one. I just hope she's made the right decision because if, as I fear, she's about to make him an offer he would be a fool to refuse, it's all over for the lot of us.

Just before nine, I make my way to the boardroom and wonder what I'll find. Only the department managers have been summoned because there isn't a room big enough in the building to accommodate all the staff in one sitting.

They nod as I pass, but I'm not interested in exchanging pleasantries with any of them. I don't care that they look worried and I have no words to reassure them, so I stand by the large window and look out over the city. Everything looks the same but soon it may all change - forever.

I hear the hushed voices of the employees and feel bad for them. I've learned over the years they are a good team and although they feared Harvey Johnson, they respected him. They must be wondering what the hell is going on and then, right on the stroke of 9, the door opens and Angel breezes into the room, looking so hot I can't think of anything other than fucking her senseless on this boardroom table.

Her blonde hair hangs straight down her back and her blue eyes look tired but excited. I know that look and can tell she's made a decision. As her gaze falls on me, I feel the blood rushing to my cock as it's always done and feel the physical ache that was left when she was no longer mine.

She nods, but I can't read her expression as she makes her way to the head of the table with Dora close behind her and I note the swell of her ass in the tightest black skirt falling just above the knee. Her tight shirt accentuates her curves and as her ass sways from side to side, it takes all my self-control not to grab her and run.

When she turns, the sunlight reflects off her smile and I see the beauty of an Angel, my Angel. She looks around the room and I can tell she takes in every expression, every look and every guarded smile of the nervous managers waiting their fate.

"Good morning everyone. I'm pleased to meet you all. You probably know already but my name's Angel Johnson and I'm the daughter of the late Harvey Johnson."

You could hear a feather blow across the floor as everyone stares at the miracle of nature that addresses them. She takes her seat and looks around at every last man and woman and smiles. "As of yesterday, I took my daddy's place at the forefront of this company. I didn't ask for it and spent all of yesterday wondering what the hell I was going to do about it. My first thought was to sell out and to be honest, I'm not sure if that idea has totally gone away."

I feel the tension in the room as she carries on in a gentle voice. "However, one thing my daddy never knew about me —at least I don't think he did, is that I'm not one to give up at the first hurdle. I just wanted to reassure you all that it will be business as usual, for the short term, anyway. I wish I could say nothing will change but I'm sure many of you agree that *everything* must change if we are to survive."

Her eyes find mine and I see the determination in hers as she says firmly, "The world no longer considers plastic as acceptable. In fact, it's increasingly obvious that unless we change, we won't have a business going forward. Now, I don't have any answers to that, but I'm guessing my daddy was already working on it. So, I need all your help to brief me on where we're at and what the proposals are going forward. We all need to know where we stand and that's what this meeting's about. I want to lay my cards out on this table and ask for your help. One thing that's become obvious to me over the short time I've been here, is that my father valued his staff. His business was his passion and meant everything to him. I'm only just realizing how strong a man he really was and although I may not understand his choices in life, I respect them. So, if you don't mind, please can you send me a report by the end of the day of where your department stands. What you're working on, what needs to be done and any thoughts you have going forward. We need to work as a team and only then will we come out the other side. This is your time to step up and be counted because you hold the answers to my questions. Now, are there any questions before you head off?"

I sense many questions lingering in the air, but none have a voice, so Angel smiles brightly. "Thank you for coming and I'll look forward to meeting all of you personally over the coming days."

She stands to leave, and I sense the relief in the air as she walks toward the door. As she passes me, she leans down and whispers, "May I have a word, Sebastian?"

Nodding, I stand and follow her to her office, neither one of us speaking until we step inside and the door shuts the rest of the world out.

She turns and I see the light in her eyes as she grins. "What do you think?"

"Of what?"

"Of my plan to try to make a go of this."

"Is this what you've decided?"

"Isn't that obvious?"

"Not really. All I saw was somebody buying themselves some time. You may decide it's too difficult and sell out from under us. How can we trust you not to do that?"

Immediately, I regret my words because I see the light

dim in her eyes and she turns away. "Fine, maybe you don't know me as well as you think you do."

"Maybe I don't."

I'm not sure why I'm being such a bastard and can only think it's because I feel frustrated at not being able to even touch her. I don't like this wall that's built up between us, and maybe that's what's making me so tetchy.

She moves toward her desk and says wearily, "Maybe you should leave."

"Not before you tell me why you've scheduled a meeting with Moretti?"

"So that's it?"

"What?"

"You're pissed because I've made a decision behind your back. You don't like the fact I've arranged something without consulting the great Sebastian. What's the matter, feeling threatened, honey?"

"If that's what you think."

"Well, prove me wrong."

"I don't have to prove anything to you. You're the one who ran out for five long years. You're the one who wouldn't stick around to find out the reason and you're the one who joined a…"

"MC club."

"Yes, smart decision, Angel. I can only imagine what sort of life you've lived being passed around between those beasts."

I know I've gone too far when she takes a step back, as if I've physically punched her and her beautiful eyes cloud with pain. "Is that really what you think of me, that I would allow any man to use me in that way?"

I feel like a complete bastard as I shrug, "Then tell me what really happened when you left."

For a moment, nothing happens. No words, no movement and no sound. Then I watch the pride force the shutters firmly shut as she hisses, "Get out."

As I turn my back on her, I feel like the biggest fool in the world. I'm not sure why I just said what I did because it's obvious an asshole has taken residence in my reasoning. Am I jealous, hell yes, which is why I walk away before I do more damage than I have already.

CHAPTER 17

ANGEL

For a moment I'm so mad I can't form thoughts. How dare he judge me without hearing the facts? The tears spill as I think about the men I've left behind. How dare he judge them that way—any of us? If there's one thing in life I'm proud of the most is that I'm a member of the greatest family there is. Yes, it's an MC club. Yes, the men there are loud, rough and play dirty, but they are so much more than that. He knows nothing about their courage, their honor, and their daily challenges. They have lived hard lives and continue to do so every day. They are warriors and win every battle they fight. They are also as broken as I am, and that's what makes us invincible. How dare he stand there and judge us so cruelly, because when I left this town, I was lucky to find them? Maybe I did seek comfort in their arms. Maybe I did relish the attention they gave me and yes, maybe I did enjoy fucking every last one of them because he's right about one thing, Angel is a whore, but not in the way he thinks. I loved each one of them and they were every bit a whore like me. We guarded our hearts and took comfort in the physical and no money changed hands. I wouldn't change a thing that I did because I love every one of them and if he has anyone to blame for that, he should take a long hard look in the mirror because it was him that sent me there.

Sebastian's mood has taken the edge of what I consider a successful meeting. I was nervous at meeting the staff and changed my mind a thousand times over during the night but ultimately; I decided to buy some time. Sebastian was right about that at least. The meeting this afternoon is to meet Tobias and size him up. I know he's a monster. That was pretty evident in the file Ryder sent me. However, we deal with monsters on a daily basis where I come from and with my family behind me; I know he is no match for us. Sebastian may think he knows everything, but all he's revealed is that he knows absolutely nothing. The Reapers are the best there is and Tobias Moretti is about to find out what that means.

Luckily, work keeps my mind occupied for the rest of the time I have before I meet the man himself. I push away any thoughts I have of Sebastian and just pore over the reports and documents that Dora drip feeds me. With every word I read, I gain a growing respect for my father. I was right; he was worried about the future of his business and was planning to diversify into ecological packaging. Biodegradable and the packaging of the future. As I continue to read, I feel the excitement growing inside me. This is amazing; he was amazing because if I'm reading this right, daddy was about to become the pioneer for a brave new world and that world was at his feet. He has a hungry customer waiting because they are keen to find something that will satisfy the next generation and ensure the longevity of their own business and my daddy holds the key to their success.

The time flies so quickly, I look up in surprise when Dora pokes her head around the door and says, "Your two-o'clock has arrived."

I note the fear in her eyes as she licks her lips nervously, and I feel nothing but anger toward the man waiting in the boardroom. However, I also feel the curiosity burning a hole in any nerves I have, so I smile brightly, "Great, this should be interesting."

Dora looks doubtful, and I laugh to myself. This should be fun.

She follows me along the corridor for the second time today to the boardroom. We pass Sebastian's door, which is open, revealing the man himself is probably waiting for me already. The anger bubbles up inside me as I head toward the imminent showdown and I feel the anger mingling with irritation at the way he's been behaving. Well, I'll show him and my father that the frightened girl who ran away grew into a strong woman with a fuck off view on life.

As I push open the door, the man waiting for me surprises me. I didn't expect this.

Sebastian's eyes meet mine and I see the anger evident in his as he says tightly, "May I introduce, Sergio Bellini, Tobias Moretti's business adviser."

I smile and extend my hand and shake the sweating palm of a man who looks as nervous as I feel inside. "I'm pleased to meet you, Mr. Bellini, but a little surprised. I was expecting to see Mr. Moretti."

He clears his throat and says nervously, "I'm sorry, Miss. Johnson, Mr. Moretti, has sent me instead. He is a very busy man and relies on me to speak for him."

I feel the anger bubbling up inside, as I say smoothly, "Is that so." Turning to Sebastian, I say coolly, "Then maybe you should call Pamela in and I will do the same with Dora."

They look at me in surprise and I say coldly, "Yes, I think that will be the best plan. All of our assistants can then conduct the meeting and relay the conversation back to us.

Then we can spend another few wasted days communicating back and forth before any decisions are made."

Mr. Bellini looks uncomfortable. "I'm sorry Miss. Johnson but I have Mr. Moretti's full permission to speak on his behalf."

I feel my eyes flash as I say coldly, "That may be so, but I will deal only with him. You see, Mr. Bellini, both Mr. Stone and my time is no less valuable than Mr. Moretti's. We both have a company to run and I take Mr. Moretti's absence as an indication that he holds no value for the company he is a minority shareholder in. Now, if you don't mind, I want you to run back to him and tell him that I expect to see him sitting in that chair over there at the same time tomorrow, where we will conduct the meeting that was arranged for today. If he can't make it because of his um… commitments, then maybe he would like to visit me at home instead."

I push my business card across the table and say tightly, "However, I don't think that will be necessary because from what I know, Mr. Moretti is a family man himself and like me, would like to keep family separate from business."

Turning to Sebastian, I nod and say icily, "Mr. Stone. I trust the same time tomorrow suits your agenda."

He nods and I turn back to Mr. Bellini and say abruptly, "It was a pleasure to meet you. Now, if you'll excuse me, I have work that demands my attention."

Spinning on my heels, I march out of the office and feel the anger walking alongside me. Mr. Moretti has just made this easy for me. He may think he has no time to meet me, but he's about to find out the hard way what that decision has cost him.

CHAPTER 18

SEBASTIAN

Mr. Bellini looks uncomfortable and I almost feel sorry for him. I can only imagine the anger that will probably be directed at him when he relays Angel's demands.

He shifts nervously and says in a slightly strained voice, "I think you should brief Miss. Johnson on how Mr. Moretti operates. He will not take kindly to her demands and we both know he's not a man to be dictated to."

Despite the fact I feel fear tying my insides in knots, I look at him coolly. "Miss. Johnson was right to be angry. She is the majority shareholder in this business and deserves respect. Mr. Moretti is the minor shareholder and although this may be a small part of his empire, if he values it, he will attend. You see, Mr. Bellini, Miss. Johnson has no loyalty to this company. She is balancing between walking away and staying to make a go of it. One thing could sway her either way. Now, if Mr. Moretti is as good a businessman as I think he is, he will see the opportunity before him. He may be a minority shareholder now but that could change if he offers to buy her out. Surely, one meeting is worth that at least?"

I see the greed spark a gleam in Mr. Bellini's eyes and we both know I have thrown him a lifeline. However he dresses my words up, it gives him the power to present a much more attractive demand to his boss. Yes, Tobias would be a fool not to be sitting in that seat tomorrow because I've seen the plans going forward and Johnson's plastics stands to be a business worth billions in the future if it's handled the right way. I just hope that Angel has seen the same vision because she would be a fool to turn her back on it.

Pamela shows Mr. Bellini out and I head purposefully toward Angel's office. I now have 24 hours to make sure she doesn't do the unthinkable and turn her back on this business because there's so much at stake for all of us. However, as I pass Dora, she calls out, "If you're looking for Angel she left."

"Left?"

I stare at her in surprise, and she smiles ruefully. "Said she needed to let off some steam."

"Where did she go?"

Dora shrugs. "She didn't say."

I feel the irritation bubbling up inside and snap. "If she calls in, pass her to me. In fact, can you try her cell, it's urgent I speak to her?"

Dora looks worried and reaches for her phone. "Of course, sir."

I watch as she dials the number and waits. After a few rings she says quietly, "I'm sorry to trouble you, Angel, but Mr. Stone would like a word."

There's a brief pause and then she replaces the receiver. "Um... she told me to tell you to um..."

She looks uncomfortable, "Um... go to hell, sir."

I say nothing and turn away before Dora sees the amusement her words bring. I can almost see Angel saying them with her eyes flashing and her stubborn mouth forming the smart reply. She was always fiery, but that used to excite me way more than it should. We were always two of a kind, which is why we gravitated toward each other. Yes, Angel is my soul mate and the ache that's never left is now a full-blown pain inside me as I realize I'm balancing on the edge of potentially losing her forever.

Ignoring the curious stares of the staff, I make my way out of the building with no explanation. I need to find Angel, and if it takes me all day and night, I will do just that.

Like a hunter tracking its prey, I slide into my sports car and relish the roar of the beast under my control. Yes, I like to be in control and Angel is about to find out the man I became in her absence.

My first stop is her family's home. If Angel wants to let off steam, I'm pretty sure this is as good a place as any. Knowing the hatred she feels for her family, she would relish the opportunity to lay into them when she's at her most volatile. As the car squeals to a halt on the gravel driveway, I waste no time in slamming the car door and striding toward the huge wooden door.

It doesn't take long before Martha appears and looks at me in surprise. "Mr. Stone, I'm sorry, were they expecting you?"

"No, I'm looking for Angel. Is she here?"

Shaking her head, Martha looks worried. "No, I haven't seen her since the reading of the will. Is she um… ok, sir?"

I see the worry in her eyes and feel bad for her. I know how much she loves Angel and has been more like a mother to the two sisters than Mrs. Johnson ever was. "Don't worry about Angel, Martha, she is absolutely fine, just behaving like a spoiled brat."

I see the relief in her eyes and she laughs softly. "She always was single minded but then I don't need to tell you that, Mr. Stone."

I nod. "No, you don't, which is why I need to speak to her. If you hear from her, please can you tell her I'm looking for her? Call me and let me know."

She nods, and I don't miss the smile she is trying to hide. Martha knows of our history and probably also knows that if anyone can get through that hard-shell Angel's wearing, I can.

As I turn to leave, I hear the clipped voice of a woman who stirs up the beast in me. "Sebastian, what a pleasant surprise, are you looking for Anastasia?"

Looking past Martha, I see Mrs. Johnson looking at me with a hard look and know she heard every word we just said. I face her with indifference. "No."

She prowls toward me and I watch Martha melt into the shadows as she takes her place. "May I have a word please, Sebastian, in the living room."

She turns to the silent housekeeper. "Please bring us some refreshment, I'm sure Sebastian could do with it just as much as I do."

Martha nods, and Mrs. Johnson faces me with a hard stare. "Follow me, you need to hear this."

Fighting my desire to ignore her altogether, I realize that I'll have to hear her out at least. Maybe she has some news on Angel and so I reluctantly follow her inside.

We say nothing until we are seated opposite one another in the green and white drawing room that is elegantly furnished like something out of an English stately home. Mrs. Johnson sits straight backed and watches me with a grim expression before saying abruptly, "You have a duty to this family and just because my husband isn't here to see you follow it through means nothing. I am now head of this family and you will respect his wishes and marry my daughter."

I almost want to laugh but say coolly, "I intend to."

The surprise flares in her eyes as my words deflect the ticking bomb watching me. I sense the relief in her eyes as she smiles. "Then I shall begin the preparations. Anastasia has waited long enough."

"Anastasia has nothing to do with this Mrs. Johnson. You see, the person I am marrying and always was is Angel."

I sense the rage in the woman before me as she snarls, "How dare you. I will not hear another word of this. You made a promise to my husband to marry Anastasia and turn your back on Angelica all those years ago because of what your father did."

As I see the venom in the woman before me, I am transported back in time to the day I sat before her husband and saw the same look in his eyes. Resisting the urge to turn and walk away, I say in a hard voice, "Things have changed. My father is dead, his shares are in my control, and there is nothing you can do about it. We all know I never wanted to marry Anastasia; it was always Angel. What I don't understand is why your husband took against that?"

Her eyes flash as she laughs bitterly. "Because he liked to control, Sebastian. You took the innocence of his beloved daughter and he could see her love for you made her weak. There was no room in his life plan for a weak heir and so he decided to break her to make her stronger."

I stare at her in shock as she laughs. "Yes, we both know he was a bastard, but you don't even know the half of it. You see, my husband took great delight in breaking people. He started with me and then turned his attention to his daughters. He had no time for Anastasia because she lacked the killer instinct that Angelica always had. She was the one most like him and he only saw me in Anastasia."

She stands and makes her way to the window and looks out across the well-maintained gardens and I hear the years of hurt and bitterness in her voice as she says dully, "Ours was not a happy marriage. It was the same situation as yours and was orchestrated between our two fathers. I was a bargaining chip. A means to get ahead, and he took it. My father would pay him well to take me off his hands." She spins around and says sadly, "Yes, those were his exact words, spoken as if I wasn't even in the room. I was a commodity much like the ones they sold and that bastard I married seized it like the greedy pig he was. I was forced to marry a cold-hearted man with no love in his heart other than money."

For the first time in my life, I feel pity for the woman who I have always detested with a passion.

Martha interrupts us by bringing in the tea and a plate of small daintily cut sandwiches, which gives Mrs. Johnson time to gather her shattered shield around her. When Martha leaves, she looks at me with a hard expression. "You see, Sebastian, love is for the weak of heart and mind. Over the years, I saw what my father saw. He wanted the best life for me, and he recognized the only way I would truly be happy is with a man like Harvey. We may not have loved each other, but I respected him. He provided me with respectability and all the trappings of wealth that I desired. If I had allowed my heart to dictate my future, it's doubtful I would have led such a privileged life. I learned to adapt to my new life, and so did Harvey. You see, I provided him with his family life and respect in the eyes of his associates and he screwed around with his whores behind my back."

She sits and takes a sip of her tea like the Queen and says matter-of-factly, "Well, what was good enough for him was good enough for me too. Like him, I indulged my own fantasies and took many lovers of my own. I discovered the excitement of betrayal behind closed doors, and I relished every minute of it. I became a woman who had it all with none of the worry that love brings. Some may call me selfish but ultimately my father knew what he was doing and in our own way, Harvey and I had the perfect marriage."

Shaking my head, I say icily, "I'm happy for you, but it changes nothing. If you think I want to live that sort of life, you're mistaken. I don't love Anastasia. Hell, I don't even like her. It was always Angel and nothing you tell me will change my mind. You know, Mrs. Johnson, if I feel anything for you now, it's pity."

Her eyes flash and she snarls, "I don't want your pity."

Standing up, I fix her with a look of disgust. "No, you want my soul. When your husband changed the direction my life was going in, he destroyed any loyalty I had to you. He used my father's weakness for his own agenda, and I will never forgive him for that. The fact you went along with it shows what a truly despicable woman you are. You treated Angel as if she was a puppet under your control. You stripped her of everything just to make her stronger. Well, congratulations, because she is now the strongest woman I have ever met and will be your downfall. Enjoy your privileged life while you can because it won't last long. In creating the hard assed daughter he wanted, Harvey overlooked one thing."

"Which is?"

"He overlooked the one important thing that drives a person to be better. To love, protect, and nurture their loved ones at all costs. Love. You see, Mrs. Johnson, he destroyed any love Angel had inside her for any of you, which makes her job far easier. Angel will tear down this company and walk away because of that decision he made all those years ago. She will relish the fact that you will be left with nothing and will walk away back to the life you pushed her into. Congratulations, you have done your job well. You have broken an Angel and rebuilt her as the devil and now you will burn in hell for altering the course of a life that was meant to be very different. Oh, and you can tell Anastasia that I never want to see her again and the next time she turns up at my office like a cheap whore wearing nothing but her own ugly principles, she will be tossed out on the street along with the rest of the trash. Do I make myself clear, Mrs. Johnson, because I know it takes a while for things to sink into that stupid brain of yours?"

As I turn and walk away, I feel nothing but emptiness. Angel's parents destroyed any emotion I had that day and replaced it with indifference. The only one who can breathe new life into my soul is the woman I won't stop looking for until I find her and take back what was always mine. Her.

CHAPTER 19

ANGEL

Men! Why is every man in my life an asshole? I feel as if I'm constantly having to make allowances for just how fucking irritating every man in my life is, and I'm done with it. I need to breathe, re-focus and put some distance between myself and a situation I'm liable to blow out of control.

Thomas Moretti, fucking mafia asshole, who thinks he can do what the hell he likes and the rest of us will be grateful for it. Well, he's messing with the wrong woman because when he sees where my home visit will take him, he will piss his pants.

Laughing to myself, I picture his expression when he sees who he's now dealing with. Nobody pays a visit to the Rubicon voluntarily and he will know of what lies within its steel-clad walls. Yes, my home is a fortress. A place of war and bad decisions, for those outside, anyway. I slid Mr. Bellini my visitors' card for a reason. Because of the address on the front. If he doesn't know it already, Tobias Moretti will soon learn what that involves, and I know he will be sitting in that chair in my boardroom at 2 pm on the dot.

The first place I went to from the office is the retreat in the woods. Pulling on my running gear, I head down the trail and start the jog that will cleanse my mind. I need this. I need to feel the wind on my face and the clear crystal air through my lungs. I need to run away again because every time I see Sebastian, it reminds me of what I've lost. Him.

I know we have unfinished business and every time I think we make progress; he reminds me of the asshole within him. Maybe he will never understand what I've become and maybe he will never accept the changes in me. The trouble is, if I'm to work alongside him, we will need to reach an understanding.

My eyes sting against the tears that build behind them. It could have been so different. We could be married and living a happy life. Maybe have a family already and none of the memories that the last five years have woven into our minds forever. What has happened to the man I loved with all my heart because the man he is now is a shadow of what he once was? I see the pain in his eyes and the bitterness of a man who life has dealt a heavy blow. I know I'm adding to his pain, but how can we ever move on if he continues to judge me for the choices I had to make?

As I run, I take comfort from the distance it gives me from the situation I'm in. For now, I must be alone because I need to get my head back in the game. Nature helps heal the pain inside and as I take pleasure in the sound of a bird singing and the warmth of the sun on my back, I begin to relax.

Sometimes I feel as if I've been running all my life. It hasn't been easy and when I ran from my family and *him*, I ran to a hard place where I learned to feel nothing. The bikers I first met are nothing like the ones I now love with all my heart. They were rough, hard and ruthless, qualities I needed in my life at that time and qualities that caused their downfall.

When the Reapers came to silence them for good, I thought my time was up. God only knows why, but they took me with them. I was taken into the fold and given my life back. I will always love them unconditionally because they taught me what love is. Maybe in Sebastian's eyes I became a whore. I don't blame him for thinking that because I know how it looks, but I'm no whore and never was. The people that count know it and that's all that matters. At least I keep telling myself it is. I'm not sure why it's so important to me what he thinks but know in my heart the real reason. I love him. I always have and probably always will. I know he loves me too in his twisted way, but is that enough to move on with? Not for me. I want more.

These thoughts and many more spin around my mind as I run for close to three hours. I can't stop once I start and stamina has never been a problem for me. Many times, I ran around the grounds of the place I call home and sometimes I had a willing companion. We were all running from something in the Rubicon and I've lived there long enough to know that when you find what gives your life meaning, the need to run stops.

By the time I return to the cabin, I'm in need of a shower, food, and a comfortable bed. However, as I turn the corner, I can see that I'm not alone and my heart quickens even more, if that's possible. Leaning against the bonnet of a sleek powerful car is a man who compliments it completely. Watching me with predatory eyes and a hard expression is the man never far away from my thoughts. Sebastian Stone.

My pace slows as I walk toward him, ready for the showdown I see coming. He watches me through a hooded expression and I feel my pulse quicken and my breathing change, labored and hard.

As I near him, he uncoils like a spring and stands tall and firm. "We need to talk."

Shrugging, I feign indifference and stand watching him with anger in my eyes. "Fuck off, Sebastian, I have nothing to say to you."

His mouth twitches and he moves an inch, and I feel the desire betraying the irritation inside me. "I think you do, Angel. In fact, I think you have a lot to say to me and rightly so."

I make to reply, and he holds up his hand. "Save your smart remarks because I have something I want to show you."

The curiosity beats down my sharp retort and I say roughly, "I bet you do."

Nodding toward the cabin, he says huskily, "Get changed and meet me in the car. It's not far."

"What, don't you even want to come inside? That's not like you, honey, from what I remember, you always wanted to come inside."

I can't help reverting to filthy remarks to disguise how unsettled he makes me, and he shrugs. "We both know one step inside that door and I wouldn't be responsible for my actions. I want you Angel, you know that but I want you to see the man I've become, while I struggle to understand the woman I made you into."

"You really are an arrogant asshole, Sebastian. Do you really think I would be so weak as to fall into your arms the minute you crook your little finger? Do you really think you've made me the woman I am because newsflash, you haven't? The only person who controls me is myself and if you came into that cabin it wouldn't change a thing. You are still the man who turned his back on me and betrayed me.

You are still the man who is engaged to my sister and allowed my father to control his destiny, and you are still the man who judges me because he doesn't understand shit. So, fuck off, Sebastian and grow some manners because you are now seriously getting on my tits."

I turn to leave and then squeal as I am suddenly airborne and hoisted over an extremely overbearing shoulder and dumped unceremoniously into the passenger seat of his car and strapped in before I know what's happening. I make to speak and once again his infernally hot mouth covers mine and possesses my sharp tongue with his. As Sebastian kisses me for a third time, I lose my mind. I hate him and love him with equal passion. I crave him and yet detest him and allow him to weaken me at every turn. I should fight back, like I'm trained to do. I should haul him off me and punch him where it hurts, but I don't. I fold into him like I always have and allow him to own me like he always has. I was fucked by Sebastian in every way possible, and yet none of that matters when I feel his touch. This is exactly why I need to run, because the only one I can't trust around us is myself.

CHAPTER 20

SEBASTIAN

The relief when I saw Angel head round that corner hit me like a tidal wave. Thank God. Seeing her looking like one hot sexy mess had the blood rushing to every part of me that she controls. I knew if I followed her into that cabin, what happened next was inevitable. Despite her words, I saw the need and hunger in her eyes, and it mirrored my own. I came here to show her what sort of man I am. I came to beg her forgiveness and show her that the past five years mean nothing now she's back. But first, I need to show her that we're not so different after all, and the only way I can do that is to show her my life.

"This changes nothing you know."

"What?"

"That kiss. You see, honey, I've kissed many men since you and that, well, it meant nothing, I'm just saying."

"Keep telling yourself that, darlin'."

"I will and you know why, because it's the truth. You see, Sebastian, I've moved on a lot since I left and found much more exciting propositions than you. In fact, I only came to get this over with. You see, I know you need to show me something, as you put it but it changes nothing. The facts are still staring us in the face and you can't change that. So, wherever we're going, I hope it's quick because I want some 'me' time before I whip Moretti's ass tomorrow."

I let her speak because I can tell she's babbling just to disguise her true feelings. Hell, we both know that's why she carries on. She's telling herself more than me because I see the brightness in her eyes and the nervous tapping of her foot that she always does when she's agitated. I see the tremble to her lower lip and the flush in her cheeks. Angel has never looked more desirable right now, and it's with a superhuman effort on my part that keeps this car in motion because I am tempted to pull over and bring her to my lap and lose myself in the woman who means everything.

Instead, I allow the asshole in me to take over and turn the music on to drown out her words. She immediately turns it off and shrieks, "You fucking asshole. How dare you silence me with Spotify? What's the matter, don't you like the truth? I'm not one of your airhead cheap dates who just wants your dick inside me and to hell with conversation."

Laughing, I turn it back on, reverting to the cocky teenager who loved to irritate the hell out of the girl beside me. For a while, we play the game of our past and wind each other up as we've always done. Angel puts on a big show of anger, but I see the light in her eyes. I see that she's enjoying this every bit as much as I am, as it becomes the usual battle of wills between us.

Luckily, it's not far and soon the end of the journey signifies the end of our game when I pull into the lot of Blacks.

As Angel takes in the sight of the club I call home, I see the understanding dawn in her eyes. "You have got to be kidding me. Blacks?"

"You know of it."

It surprises me because only those who know the scene

will understand what this name represents. She laughs softly and says with her usual husky drawl. "It appears that I'm not the only whore in town, Sebastian."

Fixing her with a stern look, I say roughly, "It's Sir to you inside these walls."

I can see she is struggling not to laugh, but I also see the excitement in her eyes as I take her hand. "You see, baby, when you left, I made a vow. There would be no other woman until I found you and begged you to come back. This place has satisfied the physical side of me with no questions asked and no feelings getting in the way. So, I suppose what I wanted you to know, is that if any of us became the whore, it was me."

I see the tears behind her eyes as she whispers, "You?"

Nodding, I raise her hand to my lips and kiss it, savoring the soft skin of the woman I love. "I'm sorry I made you feel bad about what you became. I'm sorry I judged you because I have no right to. We are no different and if anything, I am far worse because inside these walls, I use women for sex and then walk away. There are no feelings involved from either side and yet, knowing you as well as I do, I know that feelings were what drove you to do what you did. Those men..." I break off trying not to imagine her with any of them "Those men, gave you what I could not. They gave you a form of love that I know you needed. I apologize for being the one who made you run. I am sorry for not being good enough to hold on to you and I apologize for being weak and easily led. I want you to see what sort of man I became because I need to beg for your forgiveness from an even playing field. I don't deserve you but I want to fight for you now and will do whatever it takes to make you mine again."

As I break off, I almost hold my breath. I did it. I laid my heart bare and now Angel has the power to change our lives forever.

There's a short silence and I swear I hear every beat of my heart before she says softly, "Then show me."

I look at her sharply and she smiles. "Show me the man who is known as 'sir' inside these walls. Show me your world, Sebastian and I will show you mine."

Nodding, I exit the car and move around to open the passenger door. As I take her hand and help her from the car, I can only pray that I've done the right thing. It's make or break time for me now and I hope that Angel understands this world I move around in. If she doesn't, and looks at me with disgust in her pretty little eyes at the end of it, I may as well be dead because without her I have nothing.

CHAPTER 21

ANGEL

I am so excited I can't breathe. I know this place. Blacks is a BDSM club and there's a chain of them around the country and I know what goes on inside these walls, although I have never seen inside one and it excites me way more than it should.

Thinking of Sebastian as a part of this world should shock and repel me, but it doesn't. It makes my heart swell because now I know he's telling the truth. He loves me. He used this place like I used the Rubicon. A place to hide inside and keep our feelings outside the door. A place to seek comfort and forget the past. We are no different and never were. Now I know why he brought me here, and for the first time since I arrived, I see the spark of hope lighting my way. Maybe, just maybe, we can put the past behind us and salvage something of what we once had from the nightmare of the last five years.

My heart quickens as we head through the large black wooden door. The soft lighting and mirrored hallway create a serene, calm atmosphere that I know disguises what really goes on inside here.

We approach a reception desk where a man waits, watching us with interest. He nods to Sebastian. "Mr. Stone. It's good to see you, sir."

Keeping hold of my hand, Sebastian nods. "Victor. I would like to sign in my guest, Miss. Johnson."

Victor looks at me appraisingly, and I feel my cheeks redden as I remember what a hot mess I must look. I am still dressed for running and my hair is spilling out of the band holding it back. The exercise clothes I wear are soaked with perspiration and any make up on my face wore off ages ago. Sebastian, meanwhile, looks super cool and chic as always. He's dressed in a slick dark gray suit with a white shirt open at the neck. His dark hair is short and sexy and the stubble on his jaw drives the desire straight to my core. He hasn't let go of my hand yet which should annoy me but only serves to give comfort like he always did. No, Sebastian's hand belongs in mine, it always did and now it's back where it belongs, I kind of hope it will stay there.

I sign in and the man regards me coolly, looking me up and down, no doubt wondering what the hell Sebastian is doing with me. "She'll need a collar."

I look at Sebastian in surprise, and he nods. "She will."

"What? I'm not being chained to you."

Drawing me to one side, Sebastian whispers, "It's for your own protection. An uncollared woman inside these walls is a target for any Dom on the prowl. It doesn't mean anything, just a way of showing the others you're not available. Of course, we are only here to observe but we have to play by the rules."

Feeling irritated, I just nod. "Ok, have it your way... sir, but outside of these walls nobody controls me, got it?"

I watch as Sebastian's eyes flash and he leans forward and whispers, "Relax, darlin', you never know, you may enjoy being controlled by me."

Rolling my eyes, I pull away and reach for the collar the man has laid out on the desk. Before I can place it around my neck, Sebastian takes it from me and without breaking eye contact, lifts the hair from around my neck and the feel of his cool fingers on my skin, reminds me of how much I crave his touch. He fastens the collar and his hands linger on the back of my neck as he spins me around and whispers huskily, "Perfect, then again, you always were."

I see the desire in his eyes, and I swallow hard. This is going to be tough, because wanting Sebastian will be a feeling intensified by what I'm about to witness through those doors. Knowing this is what he does for fun will only make me desire him more. I already know that because looking into those dark flashing eyes just reinforces the fact that we are going to happen and it won't be long before it does.

～

WITH SEBASTIAN'S hand in mine, we head into Blacks. The gentle beat of soft music creates a welcome that makes everything almost appear normal. I see a bar in the corner of the room, which is where we head and I don't miss the curiosity in the eyes of the bartender as she watches us approach. Due to the early hour, there are not many customers and the place is large and mainly empty. Sebastian nods and says coolly, "Two house specials please, Skylar."

She smiles politely and I see her assess me as she registers my collar and Sebastian's hand firmly planted in mine.

As she turns away, I don't miss the disappointment in her eyes and I whisper, "Is she one of your... um... you know..."

He laughs. "No, she just provides the drinks."

I feel a little surprised because I didn't miss the longing in her eyes when she looked at Sebastian, and yet I'm not surprised. He's always been *that* guy. The one the girls all wanted and the most popular at school. I suppose that's why Anastasia wanted him for herself. She told me as much, but it was always just us.

Sebastian leans in and whispers, "I should just remind you that inside these walls life is very different. If we are approached by another Dom, you must not look at him directly unless asked. Submissive's speak only when addressed and the fact you are wearing the collar should deflect any awkward questions. Just go along with what I'm saying for once in your life and just observe."

Biting back the immediate response his words prompt, I just nod. "Whatever you say, sir."

I laugh to myself as I see the lust flare in his eyes, and once again, I realize just how much I want this man. Unlike the Reapers, Sebastian feels familiar. Like a favorite coat or a comforting blanket, and with him wrapped around me, I feel safe and warm. I always knew returning here would be hard, and it still is because I am wavering as I always knew I would, and being here with him, in his world, is where I know I was always meant to be.

CHAPTER 22

SEBASTIAN

I wish I knew what she was thinking. Bringing Angel here was a gamble that could backfire at any time, but I had to. I've judged her harshly, and if we are to move on and stand any chance of being together, she needs to know this side of me. But being here with my two words colliding is an experience that could go either way.

As she sips her drink through a straw, just seeing them wrapped around it makes me imagine all sorts of deprivation, and being here is like lighting a match to a can of kerosene. Angel has never looked so desirable as she does at this moment, stripped of all the finery women dress themselves in. Looking natural and unspoilt, disguising the fact I drove her into a world she should never have inhabited. What happened to her will always be down to me and I just hope I can forgive myself because the pain sits like a hard ball of anger inside my gut at what I made her do to survive. If she'll forgive me, I want to care for her and treat her the way she was always meant to be treated—forever.

I squeeze her hand a little tighter and know it's time.

Leaning forward, I take the drink from her hand and say huskily, "Follow me."

I see the excitement flare in her eyes and she licks her lips, making me want to do it for her. Just simple acts drive me insane with this woman and I am keen to get this over with so I can re-enact the fantasies in my head that have been building for five lonely years.

She follows me as I approach another door at the end of the bar, which leads to the various rooms and alcoves that enable the members to play out their scenes. I feel the familiar stirrings as I hear the sounds of screams and moans as we head through the doors, and feel the nerves of the woman beside me.

There are a few observers who look at us with curiosity as we make our way inside. Angel stays close as we reach the first observation point and we see a woman strapped to a cross naked, while her Dom whips her with a bullwhip. Her screams are of pleasure mingled with pain and I feel Angel tense beside me as she witnesses the scene before her. She starts to shiver as the woman's scream pierces the air and says fearfully, "Why is he doing that?"

"Because she wants him to."

"Why would she want that... pain, I mean?"

"Look at her Angel. She's loving it. She is so turned on right now and that's because with every stroke of pain he delivers pleasure. Some women like to feel the bite of the bullwhip but an experienced Dom will not cause pain, merely pleasure."

Her eyes are huge as she takes it all in and she whispers, "Do you... um..."

"No, I'm not into whipping my subs."

Once again, she falls silent and I hate the fact I know exactly what she's thinking. This was a huge risk because I am laying myself wide open here. If Angel doesn't like what she sees, I will become more of a monster than I already am in her eyes. I couldn't bear to see that disgust directed at me and so, I take a deep breath and move onto the next room.

Here a woman is bound on all fours, while a Dom enters her behind. He appears to be riding her like a horse and has a riding crop that he taps on her buttocks as she groans, "Harder, master."

Angel inches closer to me and holds on even tighter as the sounds of sex fill the air. Watching others scene is always a turn on like it's designed to be and there are many willing subs watching the events hoping for a scene of their own. Inside these walls it's all about the pleasure sex can bring. It's bringing the utmost pleasure to a woman or man that no vanilla couple would ever understand.

I'm not sure if it's Angel's thing, but she has to see this. We walk along and despite the hour of the day, the rooms are filled. In one two men are pleasuring one woman, in another two women are enjoying each other. Anything goes here, and it's all done with consent and within the rules. In the brief moments the couple, or participants, are together, they are devoted to each other. There's a trust and an understanding that the only thing on the agenda is pleasure. No strings attached and no judgment. This is what this place is, a sanctuary for people who like sex and enjoy the art of it. Many couples come here and enjoy the thrill it gives them and there are many single people who just enjoy a different partner.

As we reach the end, I'm almost afraid to look at her, but need to know what she thinks. The final room shows a couple having sex against the wall, while the woman's hands are tied above her head. The man is thrusting inside hard and fast and her cries of pleasure act as an aphrodisiac that is hard to ignore. For a few minutes, we just stand and watch and then Angel leans closer and I see the excitement in her eyes as she whispers, "I've seen enough, Seb. Can we leave, please?"

She turns away before I can fully assess what she's thinking, which makes me anxious because if she looks at me with anything but love, I can't deal with it.

As we make our way back, I see a friend of mine leading a sub toward one of the private rooms, and he smiles as we approach. "Sebastian, it's good to see you."

Nodding, I note he takes in the sight of Angel's hand in mine and the fact she is collared. "I never knew you'd collared a sub. When did this happen, I thought I'd never see the day?"

"I haven't. Angel's a friend I'm showing around."

It irritates me the way his eyes instantly light up and he looks at Angel with a longing look. Addressing her directly, he says lustfully, "Do you like what you see, my dear."

Raising her eyes to his, Angel nods. "Yes, sir."

I sense his interest and it irritates me, so I say curtly, "It's good to see you, Jeff, but we should be going."

He makes to speak, but I silence him with one look and he backs off. Yes, Angel is mine and if he thinks otherwise, then he is sorely mistaken.

She almost has to run to keep up with me as I head through the club, anxious as to what waits for me outside. As soon as we reach the reception, I stop and remove her collar and sign us out before almost dragging her toward the car.

"Wait up, Sebastian, what's the hurry?"

Slowing down a little, I say apologetically, "I'm sorry, it's just…"

"Jeff?"

Looking at her for the first time, I see the amusement dancing in her eyes as she stops and places her hands on her hips. "You're jealous."

"No, I'm not."

"Yes, you are. I know that look. You saw another man look at me and knew I could just crook my little finger and he would come running."

"You're delusional."

"You're an asshole but we don't need to dwell on it."

She grins and I relax for the first time since we arrived. She's fine with it. I can see it in her eyes and she is looking at me no differently.

"You know, Seb, I can see why you like that place."

"Explain."

"Because all the men in there are the same. Controlling bastards who think a woman is there just for their pleasure. Men who want all the pleasure and none of the responsibility. Men who like to use women for their own desire and then go off and eat a hearty meal, probably also prepared by somebody else. Men who live out their fantasies and then go about their business without any baggage dragging them down."

"Is that right, then why do the women go there?"

"Because they get the same. All the pleasure and none of the headaches that go with a man hanging off their skirt, demanding they act like their mothers in every room but the bedroom. You know, I can certainly see the appeal, the freedom it gives with none of the drudgery of being with someone. Um… I may just join myself."

She grins wickedly, and I know she's just teasing. Leaning against my car, I regard her coolly. "So, you want to become a member. What would be your preference?"

Biting her lower lip, she holds her head to the side, looking thoughtful. "I think I may like to call the shots. You know, whip a man senseless and then get him to fuck me with gratitude. Maybe I'll strap him to a table and spank him relentlessly, or maybe I'll try out with a woman for a change. What do you think, would that suit me do you think?"

I almost can't breathe with the thought of her with anyone but me, but I just shrug, "You'll work it out. Do you want me to wait while you go back inside and join? I could always come back later if you fancy re-enacting your fantasies with Jeff and his sub. Just saying."

Laughing, she walks toward me and sways her hips suggestively, making me lose the power of speech. She knows she has me in the palm of her hand and is playing with me like a dog with a bone. She leans against me, pressing me against the steel of the car and whispers huskily, "Maybe you can show me what it involves before I part with any cash. I mean, I would hate to go back in there inexperienced in the ways of your world."

Then she pulls back and says loudly, "Or then again, you could just drop me home. I sure do need a shower and something to eat before I'm good for anything."

She heads around to the passenger side leaving me frustrated and so turned on its doubtful I can walk, let alone sit beside her in the confined space for the journey. However, I play the usual game and just get inside the car, turning on the engine, followed by the music and pull away.

What happens next will either be the stuff of dreams - or nightmares.

CHAPTER 23

ANGEL

I am a quivering mess inside. Wow, that was intense. The world that Sebastian lives in is unbelievable. Do people really do that? Have sex with a stranger and then go shopping? It's a lot to take in, and yet the only thing I could think of was Sebastian with another woman. It makes me feel sick at the thought, yet happy at the same time. He never gave his heart to another; he kept that part of him for me, as I did for him. When I have sex with a Reaper, it's not for love, just pleasure. We are no different, really.

Occasionally they like the kinky stuff, but mostly it's just sex. Two people giving each other pleasure with no strings attached. Maybe we both entered a special kind of Hell when I left, and maybe now is the time to put an end to it.

For once, we are both silent as we make our way back to the cabin. I know Sebastian's worried at what I think about the club and his involvement in it but to be honest; it doesn't bother me at all. What does bother me is what happens next.

We are back sooner than I work it out, and I feel like a girl on her first date as he pulls to a stop outside the cabin. For a while, there's just silence as we sit outside, wondering what to do next. My heart thumps as I realize I don't want him to leave, so I say brightly, "Do you fancy a coffee before you go? Maybe we should try to get along for the sake of the business."

I watch his hands tense on the wheel and know he is as torn as I am. "Ok, thanks."

We exit the car and I feel my hands shaking as I remove the keys from my pocket. "Well, this has certainly been a strange day."

I attempt to lighten the atmosphere because I'm not sure what's going on right now and as I push open the door and Sebastian follows me inside; I have my answer.

Spinning around, my heart flutters as I throw the keys to the table and say huskily, "What now?"

I watch his eyes flash as he throws me a look that tells me exactly what is about to happen. He knows I want him, I always have, and now, as the penny drops, I see the cocky bastard return as he removes his jacket and drapes it across the chair before facing me with lust-filled eyes.

"I like it strong and black."

His eyes light up, and I know the game he's playing. Nodding, I remove my hoody and watch his eyes darken as he sees the running vest clinging to my curves as my nipples peak under his scrutiny. Pulling the band from my hair, I allow it to spill down my back as I say huskily, "I'll be right back. Do you want biscuits?"

Shaking his head, he unbuttons his shirt and I see the dark hair covering his chest as he replies, "Just the coffee."

Nodding, I spin around and walk slowly toward the kitchen.

He follows me.

As I reach for the mugs, he's behind me in a flash. I'm trapped against the counter facing the wall and he presses his body against mine and whispers, "Maybe a little cream would be a good thing."

His lips brush against my neck and my hand shakes as I set the mug down. "Coming right up."

Spinning around, I face a wall that's built of rock-hard abs and wicked intentions, and his mouth crushes against mine, lighting the flame that's always burned for him. He fists my hair and plunders my mouth, biting, searching, tasting and owning.

Groaning, I pull him hard against me and wrap my legs around his waist as he pushes against me, the clothes between us an irritant. As I feel him hard against me, I almost lose my mind. He's here. Sebastian is here where he belongs, and it feels like home.

Suddenly, nothing matters anymore. The past, the present and the future can be dealt with another day because this is inevitable. As we rip each other's clothes off in haste, there is only one thing on my mind. Him.

Sebastian feels so good it's like a drug that I've craved forever. As I cling around his waist, he pulls away from the counter and carries me into the bedroom. Kicking open the door, he lies me on the bed and strokes my hair as he looks deep into my eyes. "Are you sure, honey?"

Wanting him is a physical ache inside, and I nod. "I'm sure."

With a low growl, he claims my lips once again and feeds off my desire. Feeling his skin against mine is the best feeling in the world, and one I never thought I'd experience again. Running my hands over it feels like forbidden fruit, and as I feel him hard against me, I crave the feeling of all of him inside. Sebastian wastes no time and kisses and licks every part of me that unfolds to him like a flower in sunlight. His hot breath on my skin melts any resistance I may have, and my whole universe centers on this moment. His tongue tastes my desire, and I unravel beneath it. As he tastes the desire for himself, he groans, "Fuck, I've missed you baby."

Fisting his hair, I hold him in place as he devours me, feasting on the impossible dream. It feels as if I'm right where I should be, and the only thing missing is Sebastian inside me. I pull him up and groan, "I've missed you so much."

A lone tear trickles from my eye as I feel the pain of five wasted years and as he kisses it away, he growls, "I'm never leaving you, Angel, it was always you and nothing will ever change that."

I hear the rip of paper as he protects us both and then the slow, exquisite feeling of him entering me for the first time in what feels forever. He's home.

Sebastian claims my heart, mind, soul and body as he thrusts inside. He owns me, he always has and as I feel him explore every inch of me, it's overwhelming. I rake his back and pull him deeper inside and clench hard around his cock as he takes up ownership of my body. I scream with ecstasy as he gives me more pleasure than a body can stand and I cling to him as if he's a dream that will become a memory in the cold light of day. But Sebastian isn't in any hurry to leave and carries on relentlessly, slamming into me as if he wants the moment to last forever. I scream his name as the pressure builds and as I explode into a million pieces around his cock, his roar is like music to my ears as he comes hard and fast, over and over again.

We are not finished.

Almost immediately, he pulls back and tosses the condom in the waste bin by the bed. Then, sitting astride me, he looks deep in my eyes and growls, "I've not finished with you yet."

Spinning me around, he holds me face down on the bed and proceeds to kiss every last inch of skin on my back, traveling down to my feet. Taking each of my toes in his mouth in turn, he sucks them all, and his groans of pleasure mirror my own. As he works his way up my body, I feel the need of him all over again as I hear the rip of paper for the second time and know he will soon be back where he belongs. As he enters me from behind, I start to pant with desire. Feeling him and not seeing him is a major turn on in itself and being controlled by him is always how it was. Yes, Sebastian is an extremely dominant male, which is just the way I like it.

He rocks against me, inside and out, until I see stars. As I feel the pressure build, I try to hold on but he growls, "Come for me, Angel."

I gasp as the orgasm shoots through my body like lightning and scream as I fall from a great height. I almost feel too weak to carry on but have waited too long for this to give in to my weak body. Rolling over, I lie on top of him and say firmly, "My turn."

I repeat the favor and kiss and lick every inch of the man I crave and always have done. He tastes of familiarity and everything good in life and tasting him is like dining on heaven. As I reach his cock, his groans are like sweet music as I take him in my mouth and suck hard. He thrusts inside and I lick and suck every inch of him, relishing in the velvet smoothness and licking every drop of what spills from the tip. Cupping his balls, I run them around my fingers and love the way he tenses and groans. "Fuck me, that feels so good."

I feel the rigid, hard taste of all man and as he thrusts harder, I suck harder and faster until he gives me every last drop he can. Taking Sebastian's seed inside me is the sweetest nectar. It slides down my throat and coats every inch of me inside—with him. I could feast on him all day because I will never get enough of him. We have a lot of ground to make up, and like the greedy bitch I am, I want it all.

His strong arms pull me against his chest and for a

moment we lie pressed against each other as our hearts bang against our chests. The feeling of being with your soul mate is surely better than any other high in life. He strokes my hair and rains feather light kisses all over my face and the feelings I now have prove to me that this was always meant to be.

Day turn to night and we stay right where we are—in each other's arms. The need for food is forgotten as we make love over and over until the early hours. Real life ceases to matter as we explore every inch of our new beginning and as we fall asleep in each other's arms, it's with the certainty that when we wake, it's with a bright future ahead of us.

CHAPTER 24

SEBASTIAN

My first thought when I wake is of her. As I look across at the perfection sleeping peacefully beside me, I can't quite believe my luck. She came back to me. Despite everything that happened, we are together and nothing will ever drive a wedge between us again. Against the odds we made it through, and I thank God for hearing my prayers—she's home.

I watch her sleeping in awe of God's most perfect work. I don't deserve her; I never did, but she's mine against the odds. As she stirs, I reach out and trace the contours of her perfect face and plant a soft kiss on those bewitching lips.

"Morning darlin'."

Her eyes flutter open and a slow smile breaks out across her face. "I didn't dream it then?"

"No. This is reality, darlin', and we're about to live it forever."

"Forever, you're a bit presumptuous, aren't you?"

"Am I wrong?"

She giggles and presses herself against me, making me immediately hard.

"It depends."

"On what?"

"On whether I can get my head around the fact I'm chained to an asshole."

"If you like to be chained up, it can be arranged."

She smiles wickedly and I grin. "So, my little Angel likes a little of the hard stuff."

"Maybe, but only with an experienced Dom."

She giggles again and I reach out and pull her against me, kissing her hard and fast. Her words mean everything to me because it shows she's accepted what I became. Maybe we will explore the possibilities together, but that can wait because the only thing I want now is to show my girl just how much I love her and I don't need any tricks or whips and chains to do that.

Over breakfast we settle into domestic bliss as if we've always been together. We fry some eggs and bacon and discuss the day ahead, mainly the impending meeting with Tobias Moretti. The fact we are both absent from the office isn't the best way to lead by example but the circumstances are special ones because nothing else matters than making up for lost time.

However, we can't put off the inevitable, and once we have showered and dressed, we make the journey into town.

I can tell Angel is nervous because she does that toe tapping thing and reaching out, I grasp her hand and say reassuringly, "It will be fine, trust me."

She laughs. "Trust a man who's wearing yesterday's suit? I don't think so."

I shrug. "They'll never know and it's not as if I've had time to go home and change, not that I wanted to."

She smiles and my heart leaps. I could get used to sitting beside her and don't want anything to jeopardize this new understanding between us.

Sighing, she pulls at her lower lip. "You know, Seb, I read up on Tobias Moretti and none of its good."

"Read up on him, where, Wikipedia?"

"Not quite. No, I ran some checks on him and we're dealing with a major player here. I'm not sure either of us is equipped to do this."

"You ran some checks. Who with, the FBI?"

Shaking my head, I wonder about the life she now leads. Who are these people she mixes with and only a fool would start digging for information about Tobias Moretti?

She interrupts my thoughts. "What do you know of him?"

"Not a lot, just that he's a player and a hard one at that. My father owed him big time through gambling, which is how he came to own the shares. I know you don't mess with him, if you want to live, that is."

"I get that, but what was he like when you met him? I'm just trying to get my head around the man behind the reputation." She sighs and the warnings sirens sound loudly, so I snap, "Don't try to understand how that man's mind works, Angel. He's 100% bastard and don't you forget it. It's probably best to keep the meeting short and sweet and just reassure him his investments in safe hands. He doesn't have much contact or involvement in the business, anyway and is just happy to collect the dividends his shares pay out each year."

I can tell my words have done nothing to deter the woman beside me, and she falls deep in thought as we speed toward the town. Suddenly she changes the subject. "I should go and see my mom."

"Why?"

"Why not?"

"Because you hate her."

"I do."

"Then why?"

"Because there is unfinished business there. What she agreed to all those years ago hurt me badly. Now we have resolved our issue, I want to do the same with them."

"Them?"

"Mom and Anastasia."

I say nothing and she sighs heavily. "We need closure on this, Seb. We have to tell them where we're at and what's happening. I'm not saying we're about to become modern family or anything but I need to put this issue to bed."

"Do you want me to come with you?"

Smiling, she reaches for my hand and squeezes it gently. "Maybe it's best I go alone—I think."

Pulling into the parking bay outside the office, I think about what's just happened. It's all moved so fast since yesterday and is a lot to take in. Angel's right though, we need closure on the past to deal with the future because if I know Tobias Moretti, that could be very dark indeed.

CHAPTER 25

ANGEL

To say I'm nervous is an understatement. Ever since Sebastian and I stepped foot inside the office, I've spent every minute finding out what I can about Tobias and how he operates. I don't like what I discovered.

Ryder filled me in on the businessman, but a few internet searches revealed the player this man is in private. He is all over the internet with a different woman on his arm in most of the photographs. He's one good-looking son of a bitch and exudes confidence and charisma. However, he has dangerous eyes and even through cyberspace I feel unnerved by him. I can see he's a man who controls and I'm guessing anyone who gets in his way is dealt with mercilessly.

Further digging into his business life revealed a string of legitimate businesses he has some involvement with. Even politicians and celebrities feature in his life story and he is usually seen at all the major events. He travels in convoy and I saw pictures of him in the most expensive sports cars and boarding his private plane. Now I see the full extent of his empire, I feel unnerved by my arrogant request for him to attend today.

I hear a knock just before 2 pm, and Dora pokes her head around the door. "Um... I'm sorry, Angel but your 2-o'clock is here and waiting in the boardroom."

I smile, but I can't disguise the nerves because Dora smiles reassuringly. "You'll be fine, he seems a nice gentleman."

Shaking my head, I follow her out and wonder about Dora. I took in her heightened color and the flush to her cheeks and see that she liked what she saw. Maybe Tobias is a charmer because Dora is no fool.

I reach the boardroom and, taking a deep breath, push open the door, glad to see Sebastian already waiting. He stands up as I enter and smiles reassuringly before I turn to our guest. As expected, he hasn't come alone and Mr. Bellini is sitting alongside him, as well as a stunning woman who appears to be his assistant. Then there's the man himself. Talk, dark and handsome doesn't do this man justice. He is perfection molded into human form. Glittering dark eyes, sparkle from a chiseled face and his dark hair as black as the night, gleams in the sunlight. He smiles as I approach and holds out his hand and as I take it, his grip is hard and firm but strangely gentle and I can only imagine the pleasure those hands can give a willing participant, as well as the pain they can inflict on an unwilling one.

His aftershave is pleasant and intoxicating, much like the man himself, and it takes me a moment to gather myself and face him with indifference.

"Good afternoon Mr. Moretti, thank you for attending the meeting personally."

He nods and as I take my seat, he does the same and faces me with a keen expression. "I was intrigued, Miss. Johnson."

"Intrigued?"

"Yes, I have never been given an ultimatum to attend a

meeting before and it made me curious as to the person who would think that was a good move."

"You surprise me, Mr. Moretti."

"Please, call me Tobias, we are partners, after all."

The gleam in his eyes unnerves me and I say quickly, "I may be new to this business, Tobias, but I want to start as we mean to go on. I didn't take kindly to a substitution because I believe a person needs to know who they are in business with. Wouldn't you agree?"

"Well said, Angel, isn't it?"

"It is."

He leans back and I hold my breath because I can tell he has something to say. "Yes, Angelica Johnson, the prodigal daughter who ran away because her boyfriend…" he looks across at Sebastian who has tensed beside me, "Chose her sister over her. That must have hurt."

"It did."

He looks thoughtful. "Then this must be very hard for you, returning to face your pain and finding you must work together."

Shrugging, I say in a flat voice, "We are not here to talk about my likes or dislikes, Tobias, we are here because we are now partners."

I can tell my words have irritated him because his eyes flash and he leans back, staring at me like a Panther stalking its prey. Mr. Bellini appears rather hot because he is sweating profusely and the woman with him looks bored as if she's seen this all before. Sebastian's face is, like his name suggests, cast in stone and I take comfort in the fact he's by my side because I'm not sure how well my next remark will be received.

"Well, Tobias, I won't keep you guessing because I had an ulterior motive in bringing you here."

Immediately, the tension in the room increases as Tobias

looks at me with a hard expression. "I want you to sell me your shares."

For a moment there is silence and you can hear a passing plane in the sky and the sound of a car honking its horn outside.

Tobias just leans back and looks at me with interest, and I can tell I now have his full attention.

"They are not for sale."

"Everything's for sale, Tobias, at the right price."

"I don't need your money, Angel."

My heart sinks because I had hoped this would be over with already, but I can see that Tobias is not a man easily persuaded.

Sebastian jumps in. "That may be the case, but you must realize Johnson's plastics is going into a period of uncertainty. The market is averse to the use of single use plastics, which is the category we fall into. Added to that, its owner and chairman is dead and word on the streets is this business doesn't have long. We are offering you the opportunity to sell while the share value is still relatively high and make a large profit on your investment. Who knows what that investment will be worth in the future even two weeks from now? It's a sound business proposition and I beg you to consider it."

Nodding, I lean forward and stare at him in the eye. "I have a buyer lined up who would have the money transferred by the close of business today. This is your chance to walk away and enjoy a healthy profit. Not bad for a few hours work, wouldn't you say?"

I can tell that I've angered him by the way his eyes flash and a hard look enters his eyes. Mr. Bellini looks as if he may pass out and even his assistant appears to shrink in her seat.

Tobias also leans forward and snarls. "Do you take me for a fool, Angel?"

"Not at all, if anything, I think you are an extremely shrewd man."

"Then do not insult my intelligence in this way."

I make to speak, but he silences me with one look. "Firstly, I repeat, my shares are not for sale. They never will be. Secondly, I do not agree that this company is in danger, if anything, you are poised on the edge of a very exciting new beginning."

He laughs at the alarm on my face, as he says in a low voice. "You see, I have also been doing some digging and had a very interesting conversation with somebody very dear to you only this morning."

The tension in the room is suffocating as he adds, "Your own mother, in fact."

The alarm bells ring, but I keep it to myself and face him with a cool expression. "I'm sure that was very, um... nice for you both."

"As a matter of fact, it was. You see, Angel, I believe in the importance of family. I believe you should look after your own and treat your parents with the respect they deserve. I believe in the power of family above everything and yet it appears it's a sentiment you don't share."

"You know nothing about me."

He laughs, but it's cold and sinister and the hairs on my neck stand to attention.

"I know everything about you, Angel. I know the deal your father made to remove your lover from your life. I know he arranged for him to marry your sister to break your spirit. I also know that he was working on something that would move this company forward like a rocket launched into space. Yes, Angel, my shares will be worth billions by the time we have finished because this company is entering a brave new world and you want to leave me behind. Well, I don't take kindly to be treated like a fool, Angel and you have just made your first mistake."

My heart thumps inside me at an alarming rate, but I don't show how affected I am by his words. Instead, I shrug and say coolly, "Then your information should also have told you that I am undecided about my inheritance. You are right about my father wanting to break me, Tobias, and for a while back there he did. However, like you, I place great value on family and believe loyalty is earned, not inherited. I now have a new family who I would die for and it is them I owe my allegiance to. I believe you understand what I'm saying because I'm guessing your family is much the same. It's my new family who will support me through this testing time and my birth family means nothing to me. So, the decision is yours, sell to my new family and walk away with no hard feelings and the hand of friendship, or stay and deal with the fact that my family controls the majority of this company and do not need the money it brings. I'm in an emotional state, Tobias, and am liable to sell up and take off and you may not like your new partners. My advice would be that you get out now while things are amicable because you won't like me, or my family, when they are not."

I grab my glass and take a sip of the cool water to try to extinguish the fire within me. I need to do this. I need to regain total control of this company because the thought of being in business with a crime family is not worth thinking of. I am doing this in Sebastian's father's memory because all the time Tobias Moretti sits across the boardroom table, it's a reminder of why my father did what he did to both of us. Ryder has already offered to buy the shares and I know I have the Reapers full support with whatever decision I make.

However, Tobias is not a man who lets go so easily and says in a cold voice laced with steel and veiled threats, "I repeat, my shares are not for sale. You see, Angel, my conversation with your mother was extremely enlightening. She revealed that your father was determined to keep this as a family business. He was so disappointed not to have a son and heir to leave it to, and had to make do with his daughters. He did not value you and so why should I? She also told me that there was a clause in the will that you couldn't sell your share to anyone but family."

He laughs as he sees the alarm in my eyes, because this was something I did not know. "It appears that I've caught you off guard, Angel. Maybe you should have stayed and listened to the rest of the will that day, instead of leaving like the petulant child you are. You see, it's all in the small print, my dear and so, when you have tired of playing with the big boys, you will be the one selling your shares and the only one who can afford them will be me."

"You, I'm sorry, Tobias, but by your own admission, you just said they can only be sold to family. How does that make you suitable?"

He stands and I watch as his companions do the same and move toward the door. Tobias smiles and I see the spark of victory in his eyes as he says in a hard voice, "Because I am to marry your sister."

He says nothing else and just walks to the door and leaves without a backward glance. As the door closes behind him, it leaves nothing but shock and despair in the room behind it.

CHAPTER 26

SEBASTIAN

The silence left behind is deafening. Angel just stares at the closed door and then says in a trembling voice, "So, that's it then."

I stand and make my way toward her and hate the defeat in her eyes, mixed with hurt and pain and something else - resignation. I hate that look on her, so I say roughly, "He may think he holds all the cards, but you are still the majority shareholder here. Your word goes, and nothing will change. Tobias is just a minority shareholder and has no say in the running of this company."

"For now."

"What's that supposed to mean?"

"Think about it, Sebastian. Why would he want to marry Anastasia? It's the company he wants, it's obvious. Once he becomes family, as he puts it, the road is open to him taking control if I'm out of the way."

"Out of the way?"

Her voice trembles and she looks scared. "Tobias is the mafia, Sebastian. It would be easy for him to arrange an accident or remove me from the situation, then he would gain overall control. This is a disaster and I can't think why my mother and sister agreed to this."

My head hurts as I see the truth in her words and say roughly, "I won't let that happen, we will think of a way out of this."

She drums her fingers on the desk, and I watch her thoughts pass across her face. The fear is being overtaken by something else, and as I watch in fascination, I see why I love her so much. When she raises her eyes, I see a different look in them as she says in a cold voice, "Maybe it's time to pay my mom that visit I spoke about."

"You, or us."

"Us. It always was us and will be in the future. We'll go and find out what the hell is going on and find a way to stop that wedding from ever happening."

As I follow her out of the building, I wonder about Anastasia. I know she's pissed that things never worked out between us, but this… it doesn't make sense. Why would she agree to such a marriage unless…?

"Do you think Anastasia is out for revenge?"

Angel voices the exact same words that run through my mind, and I nod. "It appears so."

"Does she hate us that much to sacrifice herself in this way?"

The sadness in her voice makes me stop in my tracks and pull her roughly against me. Angel is fighting her feelings in every way possible because despite the distance between them, they are still her family and it must hurt they are conspiring against her.

I pull her face to mine and say gently, "Whatever her reasons, she can be persuaded. I know you have a painful past with the people who should love you the most, but now is not the time for recriminations. You need to build those bridges before they burn forever and whatever they say, you must consider the bigger picture."

I kiss her gently on the lips and for a moment she clings to me like the vulnerable woman she is right now. As my arms fold around her in a ring of steel, I make a vow to protect her at all costs. I may be up against a formidable adversary, but I will die for this woman in my arms and do whatever it takes to make her happy.

She snuggles into me and I know she's hurting badly. However, Angel has reinvented herself into a stronger woman and as she pulls back, I am happy to see the fire flashing in her eyes.

"They won't beat us; I'll make sure of it."

Nodding, I return her expression with one of my own and say roughly, "After you, darlin', it's time to make a stand."

∼

WE MAKE the journey to her home and for once we are silent. There is no music playing and no gentle teasing between us. Angel is working out her battle plan, and so am I. It will be interesting to see what the afternoon brings because there is too much at stake for us to fail.

As I bring the car to a stop outside Angel's childhood home, she grins. "Well, here we are again but two very different people than were here last."

Nodding, I reach across and grip her hand tightly. "You know I have your back, don't you?"

"You always have, Seb."

I look at her in surprise and note the mist in her eyes as she says softly, "I'm sorry."

"For what?"

"For believing that you willingly chose my sister over me. I can see now that you did it to protect your father and buy us some time. Maybe if I had stayed, things would be very different now, so I just wanted to say, I don't need to forgive you, Seb, because there is nothing to forgive."

I stare at her in shock, and she smiles sweetly. "I love you Sebastian Stone. I always have and always will, for however long our lives will be."

I almost can't speak and fight the emotion inside me to bring her lips to mine and whisper, "I've always loved you, Angel. You and me were written in the stars. It was always going to be us and it always will be. Whatever happens with the company is irrelevant to me because as long as I have you, I have the world."

As we share the sweetest kiss, my heart settles. We were always good together and now we will be a formidable team.

After one of the longest kisses we have ever shared, Angel pulls back and I note the brightness in her eyes and the flush to her cheeks. Laughing, she whispers, "Let's get this over with because I'm kind of hoping you can show me how good we are together back at the cabin."

Grinning like schoolkids, we exit the car and head toward the large, imposing wooden door. It begins.

CHAPTER 27

ANGEL

As always, Martha answers the door, and I pull her in for a hug. "It's good to see you, Martha."

As she clings to me, I feel a surge of love for the woman I consider a much better mother to me than my own. "It's good to see you too, Angelica."

"Well, well, how touching, I wondered when you'd show up again."

We pull apart and I see my mother's icy glare stabbing me in the heart as she watches our public show of affection.

Gathering myself, I stare at her coolly, "Hi mom."

She looks at Sebastian and sneers. "I'm surprised you've got the nerve to show your face around here. How could you dump the woman you were engaged to marry for five years and take up with her sister again?"

"That's rich judgment coming from the woman who pulled us apart in the first place. What's the matter, Mrs. Johnson, are you such a sore loser you can't even be happy for your daughter?"

"Loser?" She laughs bitterly. "I think you'll find I'm looking at a couple of losers. So, what is it, did your meeting throw up a few surprises you want to check out? Well, maybe I will enlighten you, then again, maybe I'll just leave you to figure it out on your own."

She turns to Martha and barks angrily, "Martha, bring some refreshments to the living room, and don't dawdle because they won't be staying long."

I feel angry at the way my mom speaks to Martha and makes to defend her but Martha shakes her head and throws me an anguished look, so I bite my tongue and follow my hated mother into the living room.

As soon as we are seated, she snaps, "I take it you've had your meeting and now probably want answers. Well, the fact is, he's right about everything. When you implied you were leaving us with nothing, I took steps to protect our inheritance. Any sane person would do the same thing."

"You think you're sane?"

"Cut the smart replies, Angelica. Remember who you are talking to. Well, to cut a long story short, I arranged my own meeting with Mr. Moretti because as the third shareholder, I knew he was my best option."

She looks across at Sebastian and sneers. "Obviously the only other proposition had already changed sides and made his own decision, so you left me no choice. The only way we could buy you out of the company was for Anastasia to marry somebody with a vested interest in securing the shares. Mr. Moretti was our only hope, so I laid it on the line for him. I told him of your father's plans to take the company into the future and made him an offer he couldn't refuse."

I stare at her in shock and say disbelievingly, "You traded in your own daughter, for money!?"

Shrugging, she stops as Martha brings the refreshment into the room and waits until she leaves. It gives me time to let the news sink in and I look at Sebastian and see he has come to the same conclusion.

Mom hands us both a cup of coffee and says triumphantly. "Anastasia has always been a model daughter. She has always been willing to do what's best for the family and so I knew she would agree. When I explained to Mr. Moretti what was at stake, he agreed to take her off my hands for the right to buy the company when the need arose."

"The need?"

Her eyes flash and she sneers, "Yes, the need, Angelica. We both know at the first sign of trouble you'll run right back to wherever you've been hiding. You have no understanding of the business you now own and no passion for it. You will soon get bored and then where will we be? No, I did the right thing for all our futures, not to mention the many workers you now employ. So, grow up and understand that I did this for us—the Johnson family and you should be thanking me."

I stare at her in utter disbelief as she takes a sip of her coffee, looking extremely pleased with herself. Sebastian's face is like thunder and from the looks of it, he could cut her dead with one look from the fire flashing in his eyes. For a moment words fail me and then I say in utter disbelief, "Do you know who you are dealing with, mom? Do you know that Tobias Moretti is the head of a mafia network that has crime running through their veins rather than blood? Do you realize what you've done, you stupid woman?"

My voice raises in decibels until I'm almost screaming at her. "You have just signed our death warrants because if you think Tobias Moretti will just sit back and let us run the show, you're delusional. That man is wicked to the core and you have just given your daughter to him. Way to go, mom, a job well done because dad will surely be turning in his grave. For your information, I made Tobias an offer to buy him out of the business. I was going to make a go of it for all of us and realize daddy's dream of building the business into a billion dollar one. Both you and Anastasia would have been the beneficiary's because I no longer care about the grudge I hold against you. However, in your mad scheming way, you've brought the whole thing crashing down, you stupid, vain, egocentric, vapid, shallow bitch."

Standing up, I feel myself shaking with anger and don't miss the fear that now masks my mother's face as I shout, "Where is Anastasia?"

"In her room, but why?"

"Because I am going to try to talk her out of making the worst decision she will ever make. Somebody's got to try to diffuse this situation because obviously you can't be trusted."

Without waiting for her reply, or even looking at Sebastian, I storm from the room and go in search of the sister I hate with all my heart but love in equal measures. I will not let her sacrifice herself to that… monster, if it's the last thing I ever do.

CHAPTER 28

SEBASTIAN

Mrs. Johnson looks as if she's about to pass out, so I stand and pour her a glass of water and hold it out to her shaking fingers. "Drink this, you look in shock."

She nods and for the first time in my life, I see that she's a broken woman. I watch her with derision, and she shakes her head. "Don't judge me."

"Why not, you've never done anything to make me think any better of you?"

I'm shocked to see the tears welling in her eyes as she whispers, "Mafia, is that really true?"

"Yes."

I offer no other words of encouragement because Angel was right to tear her off a strip. She is wicked and was prepared to sacrifice the happiness of both her daughters for her own ends.

"How do you know?"

"How do you *not* know? It's common knowledge. You obviously just see the successful, attractive business man that the press portrays. Obviously, you don't read the harder press who often cast doubt on his business practices and throw a light on his more dubious activities. Your husband knew what he was, as did my father. Why do you think my father sold him those shares all those years ago?"

"Harvey told me he was weak and greedy and wanted the money."

My voice is encased in ice as I hiss, "He was a good man. He may have had a problem, but he was never greedy. If anyone's to blame, it's you and your husband. You exploited his position and used it for your own gain. You wanted Angelica and me to break up but I never really understood why."

Mrs. Johnson shrugs. "Because you took her virginity under this roof despite the trust we always showed you."

I laugh bitterly. "Do you really expect me to believe that was the reason?"

I watch as she regains some of her fire and hisses, "We needed Angelica to be pure. If she fell in love, it was going to be with a man we chose for her. Somebody worthy, with status and standing. Somebody who Harvey would be proud to call his son-in-law and somebody who would take the company to great heights. Not you. Not the son of a weak man with health issues. Not a scrap of a boy who couldn't drag his mind from between our daughter's thighs. No, you just weren't good enough, so we intervened. We needed Angelica to hate you, because ultimately that would make her stronger. That would make her receptive to our plans because all the time you were around filling her head with youthful, fanciful nonsense, she wasn't becoming the daughter the company needed. Anastasia is and always was the spare. She was never as strong as Angelica and therefore the only way she could serve this family was to take you off our hands. She is the sacrifice we need to make to ensure all our futures. The fact she's so dim-witted makes it easy."

I stare at her with such a look of pure hatred that she laughs. "What's the matter, Sebastian, does the truth hurt? Well, I hope it does because if we are under threat it's all because of you. If you'd just done what we asked, none of this would be happening. Your love for our daughter has destroyed us all and I hope it was worth it."

"You're wrong." She raises a well plucked eyebrow and I say coldly, "The only person who has destroyed everything is *you*. You drove Angel away because of your scheming, and you are about to do the same to your other daughter. You think you have this family's best interests at heart but you're wrong. You have *your* best interests in your sights and always have. I pity you, Mrs. Johnson, because you will die alone. Your daughters won't care because they will lead by example. You will be left to dwell upon your brutal decisions and your daughters will move on to better lives without you in it. In fact, you should have died with your husband because nobody cares for you now."

She makes to speak and I say cuttingly. "Do you really think Anastasia is going to thank you for selling her into a lifetime of hurt and pain? What mother wants her daughter chained to a loveless marriage to a monster? Every day she will fear for her life because once her husband has her company, he will have no further use for her. Angel and I will move on and be happy and guess what, we won't be asking you over for Thanksgiving? So, think about what you're about to do, Mrs. Johnson, because this is your last chance. Call this charade off and leave us to deal with Tobias Moretti."

I stand and make toward the door and she says icily, "That's it, run away little boy, just like your father. He never could stand the heat, either. Your words don't scare me because you're wrong about Mr. Moretti. He is charming, good looking and successful. What mother wouldn't want that for her little girl? So, run along and take that disappointment of a daughter of mine with you and I'll look forward to the day when she decides she's had enough and leaves you in her dust."

I say nothing and leave, deciding any words are wasted on that vicious excuse for a human being.

As I slam the door behind me, Martha waits, looking agitated. "I'm so sorry, Mr. Stone, she doesn't mean those words, she's afraid."

"It's ok, Martha, you don't have to defend her, I know exactly the kind of person she is."

Martha looks worried and whispers, "Please, follow me and you can wait for Angelica in the kitchen."

I do as she says because of all the people in this house, she is the only genuine one in it and I can tell she's upset. As I take a seat at the large wooden scrubbed table, I relax a little for the first time since the meeting. The scent of baking fills the air and Martha pushes a cinnamon roll toward me and pours a coffee from the pot on the side. "She's frightened, Mr. Stone. Ever since Mr. Johnson passed she's been lost. She never had the need to make any decisions herself and when Angelica threatened to destroy her, it sent her over the edge."

"Why are you defending her, Martha, she never has a kind word to say to you?"

I'm surprised when Martha's eyes mist over and she wipes away a lone tear that escapes. "Because she's family."

"What do you mean?"

She sits down heavily in the seat opposite and says in a whisper, "Mirabelle is my cousin. She's my father's niece."

My face must register my shock because she laughs softly. "I know, it's hard to believe, but it's true. My father was her uncle and her father his brother. They were very different people and Mirabelle led a richer life than me in wealth but not emotion. Where my family was full of love, hers wasn't.

Her parents were the same as she is now and emotion was in short supply. When my own family died in a car crash, they took me in and took charge of my life. Mirabelle and I became like sisters. We were good friends, and she wasn't always this selfish person she is today. However, when she married Harvey, it was a match made by her parents and there was no love involved. She became withdrawn and aloof, and when the girls came along, she couldn't cope. She asked me to come and live with them and I loved every minute of it. I care for those girls like my own and wanted to give them the love their parents appeared incapable of doing. So, you see, Mr. Stone, Mirabelle is just as much a victim as the girls. She knows no different and feels it's the only way. Please don't judge her harshly, she's a good person underneath it all."

I stare at Martha in shock. "You love her?"

Nodding, she says in a small voice, "I always have. She's family."

"But she treats you so badly. Why do you stay? You could have found happiness with a family of your own?"

The pain in her eyes makes me regret my words, and she shakes her head.

"I could never have children of my own, so this was the next best thing. Love always passed me by and when the girls came along, it was a different type of love I craved. You ask me why I stay and let her treat me badly? We are sisters, it's what they do. Take those girls upstairs, no doubt saying terrible things to each other. They do that because they care. If Angelica didn't care for Anastasia, they wouldn't have fallen out so deeply. You see, as children, they were always close. They shared everything and were devoted to one another. When you came along, Angelica wanted your company more than her sister's and it drove a wedge between them. It's no wonder Anastasia wanted what her sister had because she saw how happy you made her. I suppose she was jealous and didn't know how to deal with it. They started fighting and things were never the same again."

"So, you're saying I'm the one responsible for them falling out?"

"Yes, but you couldn't have known. You see, Anastasia has always struggled with being second best. When she saw Angelica grab the boy they both wanted, it was too much for her to bear, so she withdrew into herself. When her parents told her of their plan, she seized it with both hands. Finally, she would have everything she thought she ever wanted, but you had other ideas. I'm sorry, Sebastian, but this web of deceit and lies spans across decades. It's no wonder things have blown up the way they have and I can only hope that Angelica finds a way of diffusing the situation because if Anastasia goes ahead with Mirabelle's plan, it will break her just as they broke Angelica."

It's a lot to take in, and my head spins with it all. Martha smiles softly and refills my mug. "Here, take a moment to think about what I've told you. I'll go and check on Mirabelle and see what's happening upstairs."

She walks away but turns back when she reaches the door. "Please don't think badly of Mirabelle, like I said, she thinks she's doing the right thing for us all."

As I watch her walk away, I feel nothing but sadness for the women who live under this roof. I just hope that Angel has a way out of this, for all their sakes.

CHAPTER 29

ANGEL

I am so angry; I almost can't think straight. My mom is something else. How on earth does she make her decisions, not based on what's right, that's for sure? It was one thing meddling in my life, but to do the exact same thing to Anastasia is astonishing.

I head straight to my sister's room, not even caring that she won't thank me for it. It's been years since we shared a good relationship and it's all because of the woman downstairs who calls herself our mother.

Preparing for the battle of my life, I am surprised to see Anastasia leaning against her window frame as I head inside her room and without looking, says in a quiet voice, "She told you then?"

I inch inside the room hesitatingly because now I'm here, I'm conscious that one word out of place could ruin everything.

"Please, tell me you're not going through with it. Not out of fear of what I might do, you know I would always have your back, despite what's happened."

She turns to face me and my heart lurches as I see the

pain in her eyes and the tremble to her lip. "My decision isn't based on that. Whatever you think, I'm not out for some petty revenge, or to please our loving mother."

"Then why?"

She shakes her head sadly and moves across to sit on the bed, taking her pillow and hugging it to her chest as if it's the only protection she will ever need.

"Because of me."

"You, what do you mean?"

She shrugs and looks so dejected it breaks my heart. "You see, Angelica, I have always been second best to you, and there's no denying it. You were the eldest, and I always looked up to you. It was obvious from a very early age that daddy favored you over me and I told myself it didn't matter. I adapted to being second choice and tried to mold myself into the perfect daughter, in mom's eyes, anyway. When Sebastian came along, you drifted further away from me and it hurt. You were always so popular and appeared to have it all, whereas I just trailed in your wake. It went on for years and I was so incredibly jealous of you."

She laughs softly and smiles. "I don't blame you for any of it, despite want you may think. It was my problem, and I thought I had it under control. The night you left; was the night I discovered my future was planned out for me with Sebastian. Mom told me there was no point in fighting it because you had run away and the burden was now on my shoulders. I was to marry him to give daddy his heir apparent and keep you from going soft as they put it. It was my duty and the chance to repay their investment in me."

"Investment, you are their daughter, for Christ's sake! You didn't ask to be born, what planet are they on?"

She laughs and I smile as we are transported back in time to a place where we constantly moaned about our parents. We share that unfortunate accident of birth and often used to compare notes on things they said to us and it was good to have someone who understood.

I move across and sit beside her and place my arm around her shoulder like we used to. She lays her head against me and it's as if the years just melt away and we are those two children again, just us against the world.

"You do know you don't have to go through with this, don't you? I have someone who wants to buy Tobias out of the business and isn't afraid of making him sell. I will always provide for you and mom; God only knows why and you don't have to go through with this ridiculous arranged marriage."

Anastasia nods and says in a small voice. "I know that. You know, we've always fought, but we both knew it was never serious. When you ran away, I always knew you would come back. Sebastian made it obvious that he wasn't interested in me and just played at being the perfect fiancé in public. I never saw him outside of that and yet a small part of me hoped that if you never returned, he would fall in love with me."

She laughs ruefully. "I'm such a fool. I just wasted five years of my life trying and now I'm right back where I started. Second choice and without purpose."

"Is that what this is, you need a purpose?"

"Maybe."

"But I can give you a job in the company if that's what you want. You'll be your own independent woman and free to meet and fall in love with the man you were always meant to find. Not an arranged marriage with the local criminal."

She shrugs and says sadly. "You don't have to spell it out, Angelica. I can google with the rest of them and know a lot about Tobias Moretti and not all of its good. I'm fully aware he's just using me and is not to be trusted."

"Then why?"

"Because I want to break free from this ridiculous life I live. If I stay here, mom will continue to control me and I'll always be second best. If I marry Tobias, she can no longer touch me. I'll be free to make a life of my own and I'm under no illusions that involves my husband to be."

"What do you mean?"

"I expect he'll just carry on as normal and wheel me out on the odd occasions, like Sebastian did. The only difference between my past and future is that I will have chosen it. I'm happy about that because I doubt I'll even see much of him. I will be free to pursue my own interests and my life will be comfortable and hopefully drama free. Don't pity me, Angelica, because I'm done playing the victim. You may not fully understand my reasons, but know I'm doing this for me and no one else. Tobias Moretti will become my husband in name only, and I am more than happy about that. You'll be free to marry Sebastian and mom will have her future guaranteed."

"Are you sure about that?"

"Yes, why?"

I lower my voice and even to my own ears, I sound desperate. "Tobias Moretti is bad news. He may be all charm and good looks on the outside, but inside the river of hell runs in his veins. He's a cold-blooded killer and I'm worried that he has plans for all of us that involve him gaining control of the company by making sure we are no longer around to challenge him."

For a moment there is silence, and then Anastasia laughs incredulously. "You think he's some sort of mafia boss, don't you? You believe I'll wake up one morning with a horse's head on my pillow and my coffin in the corner. This is the modern world now, Angelica, nobody can kill another without questions being asked, even Tobias Moretti."

I feel so exasperated, I shout, "For goodness' sake, wake

up and understand the desperate situation you are in. Tobias may be the successful businessman in public, but he runs the largest family outside of Italy. That man is mafia and you are about to sell your soul to the devil. Don't do it, for god's sake, please, I'm begging you because I think he wants to marry you to gain control of the company and that means getting me out of the way first. When he gets what he wants, he will have no further use for you and then your happy ever after will become the stuff of nightmares. Please, Anastasia, trust me and let me handle this. I'll make sure you are safe and secure and you can live a happy life without fear."

I almost think I've got through to her when she looks at me with hope in her eyes and says in a whisper, "You would really do that for me, after everything that happened with Sebastian. I thought you hated me."

The tears fall freely as I reach out and pull her to me and stutter, "I love you; I always have. It's you and me against them all and I'm so sorry I ran and left you to deal with an impossible situation on your own."

She starts to cry, and it breaks my heart as she says in a faltering voice, "I just wanted him to love me. I wanted him to look at me like he always looked at you. For once I wanted to be the center of someone's world and not the reserve. I wanted the fairy tale, but all I got was the horror story. I've had enough, Angelica. I need to get out and if that's from the frying pan into the fire, then I may as well get burned because I want to see what Anastasia can do without her family holding her back. Tobias may be taking me from one prison to another, but I want to see what that means for me. I've had enough of this life and I want more. He's rich and, as I said, uninterested. I will make sure I travel; see places I've never dreamed I could visit. I will embrace my new life whatever it may bring, safe in the knowledge he doesn't want me and won't stand in my way."

She breaks off and I see the determination in her eyes. I struggle to get my head around what she's just told me and feel responsible for her pain. I make to speak and she shakes her head, saying firmly, "I know you want to change my mind and I know you have the best intentions for doing so. Maybe things would have been different if you'd stayed, but I doubt it. You and I both know what it was like to grow up in this house, and this is my escape plan. Don't worry about who I'm marrying because it's doubtful he will even remember I'm there by the time I've finished. No, if there's one thing I've learned, it's how to play the game and this is one I've trained for all my life."

She reaches out and grasps my hands, pulling me in for a hug. "Now go and be happy, Angel. You deserve that at least, we both do."

For a moment, we stand in silence, clinging onto the past. Two sisters who shared so much, bound on different paths. No more words are necessary because we both know where we now stand. However, as I make my way to join Sebastian, what Anastasia doesn't know is I'm not the same girl who left here five years ago. I grew up and now I'm not alone. I have a family who needs a visit because if anyone can see a way out of this mess, it's them.

CHAPTER 30

SEBASTIAN

Something changed when Angel returned and I see the fire in her eyes, along with something else. Acceptance. We left her family home after assuring Martha we would keep in touch, and she was silent all the way to the freeway. After a while my curiosity gets the better of me. "What happened?"

She sighs and tugs at her hands. "She's determined. Nothing I said would change her mind, and she's adamant she's going ahead with the wedding."

"What else?"

She looks at me in surprise, and I raise my eyes. "Something changed."

She smiles gently. "Yes, it did. I found my sister again."

My heart settles a little as I see how happy that's made her, and I wonder what went on in that room upstairs.

She looks out of the window and says with determination. "The thing is, Seb, since I came back, I've achieved the impossible. Somehow, we have resolved our differences, and it's made me realize what a fool I was to run in the first place.

When I saw Anastasia, and we actually had a civilized conversation, I realized the extent of the damage I caused."

"You caused?"

"Yes, I ran from my feelings because I couldn't face them. I never stuck around to fight for you—for us, and in doing so, led Anastasia to think she could be happy in my place. However, she's spent five years trying to fill the position I vacated, and it's damaged her more than she was already. Now she's taking this marriage as a way out and I'm solely responsible."

"But your mother, surely she must take the blame along with your father?"

Reaching out, she grasps my hand and says sadly, "They were the initial cause but I was the one who let things escalate, which is why I need to be the one to put things right."

Her words alarm me because of the adversary she faces, and she says firmly, "Let's head back to your apartment tonight. You need to pack; we're going on a road trip."

"Where to?" I ask the question but with a sinking heart know the answer already, which is confirmed as she says happily, "I'm taking you home to meet the family."

She laughs and I can tell the idea is making her happy, so I hold my reservations back and nod. "Is it far?"

"About three hours North."

"Washington?"

"Spot on."

She giggles and I smile to myself. Yes, it will be hard meeting the people she obviously holds so dear and if that beast is anything to go by, I'm in for a hard time but how can I not be curious to see where she's been for the past few years?

We reach my apartment and I can tell she's impressed as we pull into the underground car park of a sleek, modern tower block, on the more affluent side of town.

"The company is obviously paying you too well."

She laughs as I raise my eyes. "If I existed on the pittance your father pays, I'd be out on the street."

She looks surprised. "Then how?"

Grinning, I take her hand and lead her to the elevator. "We all have our secrets, Angel and this is one of mine."

"One of them?"

Pulling her toward me, I claim her lips as I've wanted to do since they last left mine. Groaning, I push her against the glass of the elevator, and she folds into me. Reaching down, I inch her skirt up a little and run my hands over her ass, pressing into her, feeling how hard she makes me. She pushes against my cock and grins, "Fuck me, I can't get enough of this."

Her hand finds my cock and rubs it hard and with a muffled growl, I raise her hands above her head and hold them in place. "Just wait until I get you home."

She pouts petulantly and I swear the rest of the world tunes out, as with a low growl, I rip her panties off with force and free my raging cock. Her legs wrap around my waist and I drive in home where I always want to be. As I thrust inside, she gasps and moans, "That's it, fuck me, Seb, own me, make me yours."

I don't need telling and as I feel her slick walks clenching around my cock, she squeezes every last bit of restraint from me, as without warning, I come apart inside her. Her screams fill the elevator as she shouts my name and I don't even care that we didn't use protection because if we've made another life here in this steel-clad fuck room, I would be the happiest man alive.

The elevator reaches its destination and we quickly

rearrange our clothing, grinning like high school kids doing what they shouldn't. As the doors open, I lace my fingers with hers and pull her from the elevator toward my apartment.

As I place the key in the lock, I feel a surge of pride as I prepare to show Angel what I've done with my time since she left.

As we walk inside, she looks at me with an incredulous expression. "Oh my God, Seb, what the…?"

She stares around her in disbelief, and I laugh. "Impressive, isn't it?"

She nods and walks around her, looking in wonder at the panoramic view of the city that's all around us. My apartment is on the top floor. Some may call it a penthouse but it was never marketed that way. Every apartment in this building is impressive and was designed to take in the amazing view outside. She stands and stares at the view of the river sparkling below and the sight of blue sky and clouds rather than roof tops and bustling streets. Then her attention is taken by the modern fittings and touches that I paid a designer a small fortune to create. She turns and gasps, "But how… this place must have cost a small fortune?"

Placing my jacket on the back of the chair, I smile proudly. "When you left, I was destroyed. I couldn't believe what happened and for a while drifted, not knowing what to do about the whole sorry mess. Then I woke up one day and made a decision that until you came back, I would work on our future. I started studying the markets and even went to night school to learn the basics. Every second of my time was spent poring over stocks and shares and learning to spot the trends. I made my first investment with the small amount of money I had saved, and it doubled in size almost overnight. I reinvested that money and kept on doing so until I had a year's salary in one month. I quickly realized I had a knack for it and started to offer my services. A few months in and I had many new clients approach me as word spread at how good I was with their investments."

She shakes her head. "Wow, Seb, that's some story, I'm impressed." Reaching for her, I pull her beside me on the couch and sigh, "Then my father died, and I had to take up his position at Johnson's plastics. Your father insisted I learn the business from the bottom up, and that took most of my time. I still found time to work on my investments in my spare time and threw myself into both jobs one hundred percent. The only time off I allowed myself was when I had to escort Anastasia to an event and the club."

"Blacks?"

She looks a little put out, and I nod. "Yes, I used that place to get rid of my frustration."

I laugh as she rolls her eyes and, reaching out, stroke the side of her face and kiss her lightly on the lips. "It was always you, darlin'. Those other women were there to serve a purpose, but they never got inside my head, or heart. Blacks saved me from going mad and made me learn the importance of control and domination."

She shivers and whispers, "Domination?"

"Yes, I learned that to fully control something, or someone, you need to understand how it all works. In the case of Blacks, I had to learn what makes a woman respond and place her own needs above mine, knowing that giving her pleasure would ultimately give me pleasure. In business, I was ruthless and controlling, learning how it worked and manipulating it to my advantage. So, between all three things in my life, I created a monster."

Her eyes soften and she shifts closer. "You were never a monster to me, unless you count the day I woke up and found my prince was marrying the ugly sister."

She looks concerned as the pain in my eyes tells her a

different story and she whispers, "However, like all fairy tales, there's a happy ever after in the end. At least I hope there is."

Lowering my lips to hers, I taste my future. She kisses me back, and as I taste the sweetness of this woman in my arms, I forget what happened before. It's what happens next that matters and even if Johnson's plastics doesn't have the future we think it will. I have made enough money and contacts to ensure ours is a very comfortable one.

CHAPTER 31

ANGEL

If Sebastian's nervous, he's keeping it to himself. In fact, he has proved to be the hardest rock in my hour of need, and it feels good to have him by my side where he belongs.

We are heading toward the Rubicon in his sports car, having left the pickup back at the cabin. Laughing to myself, I remember Snake predicting I would only be back for a visit. Maybe he saw what I was blind to what seems like months instead of just a few days ago.

"You know, Seb, a lot has happened in a very short time."

"It sure has, although this couldn't be over quick enough for me."

"Why not?"

"Because I want to get on with living our lives together with no cloud hanging over us. We have a bright future ahead of us and once this... business, is sorted, we can move on."

"And just what are you planning in this bright future of ours?" I grin, knowing the answer already. I know in my heart that Sebastian and I have it all to look forward to and it's inevitable we become a couple in every way possible.

"If I told you that, I would have to kill you."

He raises his eyes and grins wickedly, and I laugh out loud. "You stole my line."

"You stole my heart."

We grin at each other like idiots and I almost have to pinch myself. How can something so good come out of so much hurt and anger?

However, all conversation stops, as I direct Sebastian onto the trail that leads to Hell. A rough piece of ground that promises a dead end - for some, anyway.

As we make our way gently down the track, I feel nervous about what Sebastian will think of my family. They are rough, crude and unforgiving, yet love even harder. They won't make it easy for him if they sense he's not genuine and I just hope they can see that I'm a different girl than the one who left here frightened and afraid of what she would find.

Sebastian's quiet beside me and as we pass the trees that line the route and head into the yard that holds the machines that wreak fear and destruction to those they visit, I swallow hard. I'm home.

As we park the car, I see the yard's almost full. I had hoped they would be out on a job because seeing the guys in a crowd is a lot to take in. Sebastian is looking around him in disbelief and I feel edgy as he says in horror, "You lived... here?"

Immediately, my defenses are up and I snap, "What's wrong with it?"

Shaking his head, he looks at me through troubled eyes. "I'm sorry, Angel, I never realized it was so..."

"You know shit, Sebastian, save your judgment until you know the facts."

I make to leave the car angry with him and he pulls me

back and smiles ruefully. "I'm sorry, darlin', you're right and I'm quick to judge. I just don't understand this world and am looking at it on first impressions."

Relaxing a little, I say urgently, "Leave your judgment in this car because the guys won't take kindly to you looking down on them. I'm guessing you'll be thinking differently when we leave, so shut the fuck up and don't say a word, or even look at them the wrong way because those guys will eat you for breakfast, lunch, and dinner."

He grins and I roll my eyes. "What?"

"You know you really turn me on when you're angry."

"Asshole."

Laughing, I exit the car and take a deep breath. I'm so ready for this.

Sebastian joins me and as we head toward the large wooden door, I point to the sign above it.

'Abandon hope all who enter here.'

Sebastian shakes his head and I laugh. "You'll see."

I push on the door and as we enter the steel compound, I hear the noise from the bar down the long passageway and my heart sinks. "I'm sorry, honey, but it appears to be happy hour."

Grinning, I pull him after me and then drop his hand immediately and rush straight into the arms of the man making his way toward us down the hall. As I jump into the strong tattooed arms that close around me in a steel embrace, I feel the tears building and say huskily, "It's good to see you, Ty."

A deep voice growls, "You too, darlin', what took you so long?"

For a moment I just relish the comfort this Reaper has always given me and settle into his arms as I've done a thousand times before. Then he growls, "Who's the guy?"

Pulling back, I beckon Sebastian forward who looks

mighty pissed and say happily, "This is Sebastian, meet Tyson, Seb, a good friend of mine."

Sebastian looks wary as Tyson sizes him up. Then he holds out his hand and as Sebastian takes it, grips it hard and growls, "I remember the name. You better be treating Angel right this time."

Nodding, Sebastian says firmly, "I always have."

Tyson frowns and I say quickly, "It's ok, Ty, he's telling the truth. I may have run before knowing the facts but it's all good now."

"Then why are you here?"

Tyson stares at me, and I know he sees everything. They have an uncanny knack of spotting bullshit in a second, and I sigh. "My problem isn't with Sebastian, it's with someone I never saw coming."

Looking concerned, Tyson growls, "What do you need?"

"Ryder." I say the one word that gets results, and Tyson nods. "Of course, although I must warn you, he's in a bad place."

"What do you mean?" Immediately, I'm worried because Ryder is never in a bad place, although I'm relieved when Tyson laughs softly. "Ashton's nearly due and Cassie's been sent home for fighting again. He's pissed at her because he wants Ashton to be trouble free in case it sets off her labor. He had to ask his sister to stay to deal with Cassie and now Ashton's pissed at him."

Laughing, I roll my eyes. "He *is* in a bad way. Thanks for the warning."

All the time we speak, I'm conscious that Sebastian is waiting and taking it all in. God only knows what's going through his mind right now and I feel a little bad for him. At least he's only met one Reaper so far, Tyson's a pussycat compared to most of them, largely because his childhood sweetheart came back to him and is now firmly by his side, when she's not touring with her band that is. If anyone knows what it's like to lose your heart, it's Tyson, which is why we spent so much time together.

He looks at Sebastian and nods. "Follow me and I'll spare you the third degree from the rest of them. They're in high spirits because we've just had a good result in the field. I'll take you out back to Ryder's office and get him to meet you there."

Smiling my thanks, we follow him to catch up with the man who we all look to in a crisis. I'm glad we saw Tyson first because when the guys are in high spirits, it's a lot to deal with.

Another reason why I'm grateful to Tyson is the scene that's playing out through those doors right now. Where there's a Reaper, there's a girl and if she's not their old lady, she's a whore. At least that's what we call ourselves and others may not understand the true meaning of it here. It's not just the women either, the men are just the same and sharing is caring around here. No pressure, no ties and no questions asked. Just an understanding that occasionally two people need comfort in each other to get through the shittiest storm. Yes, I'm grateful that Sebastian doesn't get to see that side of me - yet.

Tyson shows us to Ryder's office and as we wait for the bastard himself, I try to curb the flutter inside. Sebastian says quietly, "Who's Ryder?"

Taking a deep breath, I fill him in.

"He's the president of the Twisted Reaper MC. Hard assed ex-soldier and Navy Seal. Special forces and the hardest man I've ever met. He runs the Reapers for the government under the radar and the others are much the same as him. Ex-military, mostly special forces and unforgiving bastards. They help dispose of the government's enemies with no questions asked and are responsible for keeping the shit out of the news. Ryder King is a man no one wants to meet and the only people who call him a friend are his deputy Snake, who you met at the cabin, and Brewer his close friend. He's married to Ashton, who is the only girl I've known him to love, and he has a daughter Cassie, who was the result of one of the whores trying to trap him."

"What happened to her?"

"She's dead."

Sebastian looks shocked and I shake my head. "Not by him. She was a drug addict and picked up some guys in a bar one night. She was found dead in a ditch."

Sebastian falls silent and I can tell he's trying to understand the world I've been living in since I left.

It doesn't take long before we hear footsteps and I prepare myself to meet the man we all look to in a crisis.

As the door swings open, I almost weep with relief when I see him enter the room with a smile.

"It's good to see you, darlin'."

I nod and say happily, "You too. First tell me, is Ashton ok?"

He nods and I see the softness enter his eyes that her name always delivers. "She's coping, which is more than can be said of me. Luckily, Bonnie's around and is taking up most of the slack."

He looks across at Sebastian and nods. "This must be the infamous Mr. Stone."

Sebastian nods and holds out his hand. "I'm pleased to meet you, sir."

Rolling his eyes, Ryder says simply, "It's Ryder, we don't stand on ceremony here."

He points toward the seats in front of his desk and looks concerned. "I'm guessing you're here about Moretti."

"You guessed right."

He leans back and looks thoughtful. "Tell me your problem."

I fill him in and he listens with a blank expression and once I finish, laughs softly. "Interesting."

I wait as I see him working things out, and then he looks at me and smiles. "You don't have a problem, at least not the one you think."

"What do you mean, the guy's mafia, of course I have a problem?"

Sebastian leans forward. "We think he wants to marry Anastasia to gain control of the company. If Angel's out of the picture, the position falls to her sister. As her husband, he would take control of the company, which could be worth billions in the future."

Ryder shrugs. "You're probably right, but I doubt he has plans to remove Angel from the situation. He's just seen an opportunity to protect his interests in a business that could make him more money legit than any he runs illegitimately. You see, Angel, Tobias Moretti may head up a crime family, but the word on the street is he's cleaning them up. You see, he's now in the habit of securing well respected businesses that require no work on his part, with maximum pay-out. He leaves the running of those companies to the people who know how to and reaps the dividends his shares bring. The fact he's made this move is indeed an interesting one, but I'm guessing has more to do with protecting the future earnings of the company, than actually gaining control."

"But what if you're wrong?"

Ryder raises his eyes and I say quickly, "What if he decides that he wants me out of the way? I don't think I can live under the pressure of waiting for something to happen; it's too much, Ryder. What with everything that's going on and the fact my sister could be in danger herself, I just want him out of the picture."

Leaning back, Ryder nods and I watch his expression soften. It's an unusual sight and I think I hold my breath as he leans forward and stares me right in the eye.

"You're a Reaper, Angel and nobody messes with us. Now it's up to me to make sure Moretti knows that."

"What are you going to do?"

Ryder narrows his eyes and the tension immediately increases in the room. "Pay him a visit."

Almost as if they have a sixth sense, the door opens and Snake and Brewer enter the room. Jumping up, I hug each one in turn and Snake grins. "I told you you'd visit."

He looks at Sebastian and holds out his hand. "Take care of her or I'll be seeing you."

Sebastian nods. "Then I *won't* be seeing you."

Laughing, Brewer hugs me and winks. "So, Angel's leaving us."

His words cause the tears to fall as I realize what that means. It's one thing living here and being part of their world where everything is safe and easy, and I'm not sure if I'm ready to take on the responsibility of the world outside these walls. Suddenly, a strong hand pulls me back and into the arms that I know I belong in. Sebastian says firmly, "I'll look after her. You have my word on that."

Ryder's voice cuts through the emotion in the room as he growls, "Snake, grab about ten of the men, we've got a visit to make."

Snake grins and I roll my eyes. God, that man thrives on conflict. However, I feel anxious and it must show because Ryder laughs. "Chill, Angel, it won't be the first time we've had the pleasure of meeting Moretti. This time it's personal though. Leave it with us and take the time to catch up with the others. Show Sebastian who Angel is now and just relax knowing we're dealing with it."

He jumps up and reaches for his battered leather jacket

from the chair next to his desk and, as he slips it on, a lump forms in my throat. Heading across, I reach up and kiss him on the cheek and whisper, "Thank you."

He winks and then grins. "Any excuse to get some peace. My sister is seriously pissing me off and I'm liable to be much more of a danger to the people here than I will be to Moretti. You've just done me a favor, honey, now go and introduce your man to the rest of them."

We follow them out and I take Sebastian's hand and squeeze it reassuringly. Maybe now he's met Ryder, the rest won't be such a shock. Then again, maybe not.

CHAPTER 32

SEBASTIAN

I'm not sure I'm ready to meet Angel's 'family' as she calls them. The men I've met so far remind me of the hell I sent her to and even though I see the love they have for her; I still can't help feeling responsible for breaking Angel so badly.

She leads me toward the noise coming from a door at the far side of the hall and I prepare myself for not liking what I see inside. However, before we reach it, we hear a loud, "Angel!"

Turning around, I see a stunning woman heading toward us, looking so happy, sweet and heavily pregnant, and I realize this must be Ryder's wife, Ashton. Walking with her is another stunning woman with long red hair and stunning eyes and she looks just as happy to see Angel, who squeals and runs into their outstretched arms.

As I wait patiently for their hugs to end, I look at the women who appear to be very out of place in this rough environment because they look - normal.

After a lot of excited chatter, Angel turns and pulls me forward. "Sebastian, meet Ashton and Bonnie. You've already met their old men, so you may as well see where the real power lies in this place."

I'm won over immediately by the warm smiles and looks of mild curiosity the women give me and Ashton says in a soft southern drawl, "We've heard a lot about you, Sebastian, it's good to finally meet you."

I note the sharpness in Bonnie's eyes and wince a little before smiling. "Hopefully the things you hear in the future will be a lot more flattering."

Angel laughs softly and slips her hand in mine. "It's all good. Sebastian has suffered just as much as me, but it's all in the past now."

The women look happy for her and Ashton says sweetly, "We were just heading to the bar to chill out for a bit. Ryder's sister's sitting Cassie and as he's been called away, we thought we'd get some peace for once."

Angel looks at her guiltily. "I'm sorry, I'm the cause of that, I hope you don't mind."

Laughing, Ashton, and Bonnie share a look. "We should be thanking you, honey. Ryder's been impossible these past few days, and all his fussing is seriously pissing me off. I can't do a thing without him trying to interfere, and it's making me stir crazy. Thank god for Bonnie, she's the only sane one in this place I can count on to keep it real."

Bonnie rolls her eyes. "Those men may be hard bastards but their clueless to normal life. No, we're making a night of it, although Ashton's sticking to the soft drinks, but I intend on getting wasted."

"While the cat's away…" Angel laughs and the girls all share a look that shows the bond they share that outsiders will never understand.

Bonnie looks at me and shakes her head. "I don't envy you."

"Why?" I feel surprised and a little worried, but she laughs softly. "The first time an outsider ventures into the Reaper's den, it can be a lot to deal with. They're good guys and girls, so don't be put off by what you see."

The alarm bells ring and I can tell that Angel is nervous beside me. Bonnie and Ashton throw her a pitying look, which only increases my anxiety.

They walk with us and I still can't believe these two women live here and look as if this is normal.

As we reach the door, the girls smile reassuringly and Angel takes my hand and appears to take a deep breath. "Are you ready for this, Seb?"

I squeeze her hand and whisper, "Nothing can change how I feel about you, darlin', you know that."

She looks unconvinced, and as the door opens, the noise that hits us drowns out any further conversation.

All around us are bikers. Huge, ferocious looking men all with one thing in common. The tattoos they wear on their muscle-bound bodies and their fuck-off attitude. It makes me shiver just looking at them because you wouldn't want to meet *one* of these men on a dark night, let alone what must be around thirty of them. They are positioned around the room, either laughing in groups or playing pool or cards. A huge bar dominates one end where I see various women with a drink in hand and if they aren't chatting among themselves, they are pressed against one of the men or sitting on their laps. It's like a scene from a violent movie as the guys party hard and the women appear to love every minute.

It doesn't take long for them to notice Angel and I hear calls of, "Angel, honey, good to see you."

I try not to let it show how disturbed I am, as one by one they envelop her in a hug and throw me an appraising look. I feel their curiosity mixed with a hard look as they work out the relationship between me and the woman they obviously care a lot about. Angel tries to introduce me, but their names are soon forgotten as another one is added to my memory. The girls shriek and swamp Angel with kisses and questions and they too assess every inch of me as I wait patiently beside Ashton and Bonnie, who act as the sweetest type of bodyguard.

I try not to judge, but I see in an instant what goes on in this place. The men are crude and the women appear to love it. The air is supercharged with testosterone and sexual energy and, unlike Blacks, there is no restraint. The alcohol flows and the jokes are blue and the women have pure excitement in their eyes as the men surround them. This is one big party that's certain to end in the bedroom and my heart hurts at the knowledge this is how Angel existed for five years. Thinking of her with even one of these men is bad enough, but knowing that she's probably been with most of them is a lot to take in and yet I am no different. I too have lost track of how many women I've had sex with and I should judge myself more harshly because there was no love in my heart for any of them. I can tell that Angel holds a heart full of love for these guys and so, I suck it up and smile as she tries to introduce me to her life.

Once the initial excitement at her return subsides, we head toward the bar with Ashton and Bonnie, who laughs. "Well done, Sebastian, you dealt with that well."

Pulling up stools, Ashton groans as she tries to make herself comfortable and Angel looks concerned. "How long?"

"Two weeks, but to be honest, I hope he's early."

"He?"

She grins and Angel's face softens and I can see why Ryder is so overprotective of her. This woman has a softness and vulnerability that would make a man kill an army to protect her. She is sweet and almost innocent, but there's a hint of steel running through her that shows she's no pushover.

She says softly, "Yes, a little boy. We are undecided on a name but I'm sure when the little guy makes an appearance, it will all slot into place."

Bonnie laughs. "The guys have a sweepstake. Snake thinks it will be Titan."

Rolling her eyes, Ashton laughs. "He's lost then."

Angel laughs and I wonder about these women. It seems such a violent place to bring a small baby to and Angel must sense my concern because she leans in and whispers, "I'll show you around later, you'll understand then."

A girl who is serving drinks behind the bar approaches and looks at me with curiosity. She grins at Angel and laughs, "You were right about him, honey - gorgeous."

Feeling my lips twitch, Angel groans. "Ok Millie, don't give him a bigger ego than he has already. It's good to see you, by the way, don't I get a hug from my best friend?"

Unlike the other greetings, I can tell these girls love each other very much as they hug it out across the bar. I can sense the emotion as they hold on to each other and Bonnie whispers, "Millie is Angel's best friend here. She's missed her terribly, even though it's not been long. The single girls here rely on each other more than most because they understand only too well what it's like living in this madhouse."

I look with interest at the two women and note the love in Millie's eyes for the woman who has left this life for, hopefully, a better one. It must hurt losing a close friend, and I feel a surge of sympathy for the pretty girl.

Millie pushes a cool beer toward me and I eavesdrop on their conversation while Ashton and Bonnie talk about babies.

Millie points to a man in the corner of the room. Something about that particular man strikes fear in my heart because, like most of the guys here, he is built like a machine. He is pumped and ripped and the tattoos on his arms are stretched against his skin and his t-shirt is doing a bad job of covering him. His hair is dark and fairly long and there's a scar running above his left eye. The look he wears is of grim determination as I watch him throw his hand of cards down on the table and hear his companion growl, "Fuck me, Mav, again - this is getting old."

The guy grins and I watch his eyes flash as he sweeps the dollars toward him and grabs his beer, taking a long swig before setting it down. Then his eyes scan the room and land on Millie and the look in them tells me exactly what he wants from her. Millie gasps and whispers to Angel, "Looks like my lucky night; you're staying, aren't you, please say you are. We need to catch up properly?"

Angel looks across at me and smiles tentatively and I nod, "If you want to, that's fine by me."

She smiles, and it's as if the sun comes out and I know I can deny her nothing. She always was and always will be my number one priority and if being here makes her happy, then, reluctantly, so am I.

We watch Millie head across to the giant of a man in the corner and he pulls her effortlessly onto his lap and runs his hands around her tiny waist. She snuggles into him and appears to be more than happy to be there, and Angel laughs softly. "That's made her day."

She leans forward and whispers, "That's Maverick. He's a cold bastard with apparently no feelings. Don't get me wrong, they're all like that but he's worse than most."

Bonnie leans forward. "I hear you mention Maverick. Word is, Ryder's got plans for him. Apparently, some politician's daughter in danger and Ryder thinks Mav might be the man for the job."

Angel almost spits out her drink. "You have got to be kidding! Maverick guarding a politician's princess, why would anyone think that's a good idea? He'll probably kill her himself just out of irritation."

Ashton laughs. "Who knows how Ryder's mind works, he's usually right though?"

She smiles and by the look in her eyes, she's thinking about her husband and I can see immediately the huge love she has for him.

Angel laughs and then leans in and whispers, "Let me show you around. It will all make a lot more sense then."

She says goodbye to the others and as I follow her out, I'm not sorry to leave the room. Although the people in it were friendly enough, I could sense their mistrust of me and general unease. I'm guessing Angel told them what happened to make her come here and know I'll have to prove my worth before any of them accept us as a couple.

The slamming door cancels out the noise and Angel giggles. "Sorry, Seb, that was intense. At least you've met them now."

She slips her hand in mine and pulls me toward her and kisses me softly on the lips. "Thanks though. I know it took a lot for you to face them and it means the world to me seeing all the people I love in the same room. Anyway, before I show you my room, I'll show you what makes this place a home."

For the next hour, Angel shows me around the steel-clad prison that houses this strange crowd. As we walk outside, she points out various modern sleek houses in the clearing. "That's where the married Reapers lived with their families. They live in a community and watch out for each other. Once a Reaper takes an old lady, they live a relatively normal life. The kids all play together and go to school in the town nearby. They are brought up to respect and love in equal measures but are also taught to take no shit and stand up for themselves. In fact, we all are."

"What do you mean?"

She grins. "We are taught to fight, defend ourselves and not be a victim. Most of us came here because we were running from something, but the guys teach us to stop running and stand our ground. The women play a huge part in that too, rebuilding shattered confidence and providing a friendly wise ear when we need to offload."

She looks a little guilty. "They know everything about my past, Seb. They know what brought me here and why I ran. They know the bad and the good and they helped me make sense of it all. Then they made me into a stronger woman, which gave me the courage to come back and face you all. I owe these people everything because they proved more like a family than mine ever did and it's important to me that you understand they will always be in my life."

As I look around at Angel's home, I finally begin to understand just how special this place is.

CHAPTER 33

ANGEL

Coming home made me realize just how much I love this place and everyone in it. Coming home with Sebastian made everything right with my world. I wanted to show him who I became, and it's important to me that he understands who I am now and doesn't judge me. If I had to choose between the two entities, The Reapers or him, I'm not sure he would like my decision. However, what I also realized in coming here was how much I love him.

Seeing the other guys was great, but nothing like I feel when I'm with him. Yes, Sebastian was always my soul mate, and that never changed. When Millie was excited to spend time with Maverick, I was happy for her. She has always liked him and I know he will treat her well, at least for one night. You see, that's what it is here. One night of love and more excitement than a woman can stand and then maybe a month will go past before that same Reaper comes calling. If Millie is harboring feelings for Maverick, she would do well to forget them. That man is and probably always will be, a cold hard bastard who ditched any feelings inside him a long time back.

After I show Sebastian the gym and pool and the communal kitchen, I head toward the block of apartments near the main house where the whores live.

As we head inside, I breathe in the familiar smell of perfume that lingers in the air and sigh happily. Turning to Seb, I smile. "It feels good to be back."

I note his concern and shake my head. "This will always be my home, but I'm guessing I'll have to vacate my room in case someone else needs it. They have visitors' rooms though, so we will always have a bed here."

Seb smiles and pulls me close. "You can come back here whenever you want to. You know I understand your love for this place and I'm not going to get in the way of that. However, know that I am going to do everything I can to make you happy and if that means coming here with you, then you just have to say the word."

My heart leaps and I feel the love drowning the doubts and crushing them forever. Pulling away, I grin with excitement. "Come on, I'll show you my own particular piece of paradise."

Dragging him up the flight of stairs and along the hall, I stop outside the familiar door and take the key from my purse. "Honey, we're home."

Laughing, I push open the door. "You know, Seb, you're honored."

"Why?"

"Because no man has ever set foot in here with me."

He looks surprised, and I giggle at his expression. "Strictly a 'no man' zone. This was my personal sanctuary and you can relax knowing how special you are."

His eyes flash and I know that look as he takes two steps and covers the short distance between us before pulling me roughly against him. "So, no man has ever kissed you here."

He lowers his lips to my neck and I shiver. "No."

"And no other man has ever done this—here?"

He lifts my top off and kisses my quivering chest.

"No." My voice is husky and I feel so turned on I almost can't breathe.

"And no man has ever touched you here?"

He cups my breast and rolls his thumb around the nipple as it reacts to his touch. "No."

As his lips crash against mine, the heat travels through my body. Then with a low growl, he makes short work of removing every last item of clothing on both of us and pulls me against him. The feel of his skin against mine is like a velvet glove, caressing me and sending little messages of lust throughout my body. He pulls me toward the bed and lowers me gently down, and proceeds to kiss me all over as I tremble with anticipation. As he licks, teases and demands my body to react to his touch, I lose myself in desire for him. His hard chest would rival any Reapers, and the hardness between his legs is more than a match for any other. As Sebastian makes love to me, I feel like a princess. He worships me like any girl would wish to be and as he enters me hard and fast, thrusting home where he's always been destined to live, I thank God for happy ever afters and know that now my future is a bright one with the man I have always loved.

~

THE SUN POURS through the crack in the drapes and I look across at the man sleeping peacefully beside me. As I stare at him, I feel like the luckiest woman alive. He stirs and as he opens his eyes, I see the lust in mine mirrored right back at me. Without saying a word, I reach across and kiss him softly on the mouth. Then I move down his body, kissing every inch of skin with soft feather like kisses, and drag my tongue across his chest. As I reach his thighs, he groans and his cock reminds me of what I want and as I lick the tip, he growls, "Fuck…"

Silently, I take his velvet shaft in my mouth and suck gently, loving the way he tenses and groans with desire. My hands massage his balls and as I dig my nails in, he thrusts inside to the back of my throat and I suck harder. I feel so powerful as the dominant man under me jerks and groans with desire and I rub my breasts against him, loving the way the hardness against my skin ignites the fire within me. He makes to pull me up, but I resist and suck even harder. When I can feel he is close, I position myself above him and lower myself gently down onto his hard cock and rub my clit against it, groaning as I feel the friction between us. He growls as I tease him by taking my time and he reaches up and fists my hair in his hand and pulls me roughly down and kisses me relentlessly. As I rock back and forth, he stretches me in an intoxicating way and I gasp as my clit drags against his shaft. I feel my desire coat him, my orgasm building like a storm waiting to break and just before it does, he rolls me over on my back and grips my arms, pinning me down as he thrusts inside like a wild animal. As he enters me, he growls, "You're mine, Angel, no one else."

I gasp, "I always was."

As Sebastian explodes inside me, the force of it causes me to shatter into a million pieces under him. As the sweat from my body joins his and our bodies cement us together, I have never been so happy in my life.

Remaining inside me, Sebastian strokes my hair and says huskily, "I love you, Angel, I always have."

My voice trembles with emotion as I say the words I have never stopped believing in. "I love you, Sebastian Stone and I can't wait to see where that takes us."

He appears in no hurry to leave my body and for a while

we just lie joined together, sharing soft kisses and scorching looks. Then nature evicts him and as he rolls onto his back, he laughs softly. "What?"

"You know, your daddy would turn in his grave he saw us now—especially here."

"Hmm, I expect he would, but not half as much as he will when he sees what mom has planned for Anastasia."

Looking concerned, Sebastian turns to face me. "Do you think Ryder can sort it?"

"I'm not sure - probably. I mean, only someone with a death wish goes against the Reapers, but I kind of got the impression Ryder wasn't bothered by Moretti. They should be back now. Maybe we should grab some breakfast and head over and see what happened."

Sebastian nods and reluctantly we leave the warmth of the bed and head for the shower. As we do, I feel the unease returning as I think about the fate that awaits us all if Moretti goes through with his threat to marry Anastasia. Whatever anyone says, I know it will end in disaster for us all, and I just hope Ryder diffused the ticking time bomb that's threatening to blow our worlds apart.

CHAPTER 34

SEBASTIAN

Angel fixes us croissants and coffee in their communal kitchen and for a while we are the only ones here until a bleary-eyed Millie enters the room looking wrecked. Her face lights up when she sees us watching her with amusement and she grins sheepishly, "Well, who can blame a girl?"

Angel laughs and as Millie grabs a coffee from the pot, she teases, "Somebody didn't get much sleep last night."

Millie winks and I feel the pain hit my heart as I see this is a conversation they probably shared most days and that time it involved Angel.

Millie sighs and sits opposite. "You know, he's a strange one."

"Why?" Angel looks interested and Millie rolls her eyes. "He doesn't give anything away. He keeps those emotions firmly inside and just uses them to give a girl more pleasure than she should ever be able to stand. He's a machine and to be honest, I'm wrecked. Him though, he was up at 5 and in the gym punishing the machines in there. Last I saw, he was heading out for a run and I doubt we'll see him until he's completed his usual ten kilometers. I'll never understand these guys, surely they're not human."

Laughing, Angel takes a bite of her croissant and Millie sighs. "You're lucky, babe, at least you found your happy ever after. I'm not sure I'm ready for mine yet because god knows this place is like a hard drug that I'll probably never kick the habit. Man, I feel like the luckiest girl alive."

Angel giggles and they are soon gossiping about some woman called Vanity. I tune out as I try to get my head around the world they live in. It's like some form of fuck academy and I thought Blacks was bad. Thinking of Blacks makes me hard all over again and for a different reason this time. As soon as this shit is over, I'm going to show Angel just what makes a dominant tick and I will enjoy dominating my beauty because it's been a long time coming. Yes, by the end of it, she will submit to me and love every minute of it.

Thoughts of the pleasure I'll give her make it difficult to concentrate on anything else, but suddenly, she turns to me and says with a worried look, "I think we should go and find Ryder. You know, if Anastasia is still going through with this, then we may be needed back at home to try to change her mind."

Millie's eyes fill with tears. "But you've just arrived."

Angel reaches across and hugs her, saying gently, "Come and stay with us, babe. As soon as we sort things out, there's a bed waiting for you. It's not far and we'll still be close, we always will."

"It won't be the same though, it sucks not having you here."

I see the pain inside them and feel bad. It appears they share a much closer relationship than Angel does with her own sister and so I say firmly, "Angel's right. There will always be a place for you with us. You are always welcome."

Millie smiles gratefully and then says loudly, "I'm off to get some sleep. I can't stand goodbyes, so until I see you next, take care of yourself."

She faces me with a firm expression. "Look after her, Sebastian. If you don't, I'll be after you, you have my word on that."

Grinning, I nod and grab hold of Angel's hand and pull her against me. "And you have my word she's in safe hands. She is my number one priority and I won't ever forget that."

Millie smiles and heads off, and Angel sighs. "I feel bad for leaving her, but we have a job to take care of. Let's go and see what the score is."

∽

IT DOESN'T TAKE LONG for us to reach Ryder's office and Angel knocks gently on the door. Almost at once we hear a terse, "Come in."

Rolling her eyes, Angel smiles reassuringly and we head inside. I balk at the sight of Ryder sitting with his feet on the desk with Snake in the chair across from him and Brewer on the couch in the corner. There is a half-bottle of whiskey on the desk and the glasses they raise to their lips are almost empty. Their eyes are bright and I sense they haven't been to bed because they look weary and as if they could use a shower and a decent night's sleep.

Angel looks worried, and Ryder growls. "Sit."

We sit beside Brewer, who rolls his eyes and Angel looks at Ryder nervously. "What happened?"

I can tell she's nervous, which makes me nervous and Ryder shakes his head. "We just got back. Moretti was on his way out when we got there and wasn't in any mood for unwelcome visitors."

I sense Angel's fear, but then Snake laughs. "He had no choice though."

Brewer nods, and Ryder grins. "They are never happy to see us and that's always part of the fun."

The guys laugh and yet Angel still looks worried. "Did you sort it, will he sell?"

Ryder shakes his head. "No, he told us he will never sell because those shares stand to make him billions in the future. He did assure us of his intentions toward you and your sister."

"Which are?" her voice sounds fearful and I reach for her hand, squeezing it reassuringly. "Moretti isn't interested in Johnson's plastics. He just wants the dividends and is happy for you to run it, however…"

Ryder leans forward and narrows his eyes. "He wants to marry your sister to protect his investment."

"But why, we could always draw up a contract to offer him first refusal on the shares if I wanted to sell?"

Snake laughs and they share a look. "The thing is, darlin', Moretti has seen this marriage as a way of solving a few of his own problems. Apparently, he's been looking for a wife who will help portray him more as a respectable businessman. His marriage, as he puts it, is purely a business arrangement and nobody is forcing anyone to do anything they don't want to."

Ryder nods. "We made it clear that your protection was our top priority and if anything happened to you, or your family, we would be paying him another unfriendly visit. He gave us his word he has no plans to hurt any of you and just wants what's best for business. You know, Angel…" Ryder leans back and raises the glass to his lips, throwing the remains down the back of his throat. "It's better to keep your enemies close. In this case, Moretti is better with you than against you. If what you say is right and that Johnson's plastics is set for a bright future, you would be the target of every business shark out there. With him involved, they would be fools to try. He has a small share and appears happy with that. My advice would be to see how it goes and keep us informed of any developments. Moretti may be mafia, but like I said before, he is aware that things need to evolve and change. If anything, I respect the man because he is trying to redesign an age-old institution and clean it up into a business machine. You will do well out of the association and if things change, we will reassess the situation."

Although his words reassure me, I can tell that Angel is still worried. She tugs on her hands and bites her bottom lip and Brewer reaches across and grasps her other hand. "Listen, darlin', push away that worry because that's what we're here to do on your behalf. It was a good meeting and we're just tired from the ride. Go home and start your life knowing we have your back. Come back to visit though because we miss you and want to hear how it's all going."

Ryder nods. "Brewer's right, there's nothing you can do except get on with your life. We'll miss you though, so come back lots, otherwise we'll be coming to find you."

They laugh and Angel relaxes for the first time since they started their conversation and her voice breaks as she whispers, "Thanks Ryder, guys…"

Her voice is laced with emotion and Snake growls, "I'm heading off to bed. I hate this personal shit."

We all laugh and Ryder groans. "I'm back to face my sister, who by all accounts is pissed because I left Ashton last night. You should see the fucking messages she's sent me."

We all laugh and as we stand, Ryder does too and holds out his hand. As I take it, he grips mine tightly and growls, "Look after her."

"I will, you have my word on that."

As I watch them say their goodbyes, I feel a little envious of the relationship they all share. It appears I was wrong in judging them so harshly because who wouldn't want to be part of this?

CHAPTER 35

SEBASTIAN

"Mom, Anastasia!" Angel shouts as we enter the house, which is our first stop since leaving the Reaper compound.

Martha appears with tears in her eyes and says with relief, "Angelica, thank goodness you're here."

Angel looks worried and Martha shakes her head. "They left already."

"Left... where?"

"Mr. Moretti came, and they left with him and a lot of other people. There must have been about three cars and a few motorbikes. Your mom made me pack everything of Anastasia's because she told me she wouldn't be back."

"What did she mean?"

Angel looks so worried I interrupt. "Where did they go?"

"The Church, you just missed them."

I make to leave and Angel says abruptly, "What's going on?"

"We're going to stop them."

Martha looks concerned. "I think you should save yourselves the trouble. I spoke to Anastasia and her mind's made up. There's nothing anyone can do to talk her out of it."

Angel's eyes fill with tears and Martha's expression softens. "Listen, honey, sometimes you have to let someone go in order for them to fly. Anastasia is unhappy here and has been for some time. Your mom's a hard woman to live with, you know that, and maybe Anastasia sees this marriage as a solution to her problems. Leave her to make her own mistakes because she won't thank you for interfering. Just be there for her when she needs you and be happy for her if she's happy. You never know, it may be the making of her."

"Or the end."

Angel sounds bitter and Martha smiles. "You should know more than most what it's like living with monsters in disguise. There's always a ray of hope in every situation and you just have to trust that Anastasia will find it in hers. Now, go and change, your sister needs you."

~

BY THE TIME we're ready I think we've been home for just ten minutes and as we say our goodbyes, Martha hugs Angel warmly and says with emotion laced through her voice, "Don't judge your mom. She does what she thinks best and doesn't mean harm by it."

Pulling back, Angel says irritably, "You always defend her and yet she treats you like shit most of the time. Maybe you should think about leaving and finding yourself a decent employer. You know, I will always give you a job."

She turns to me and her eyes sparkle, "What do you say, honey, when we find a home together, can Martha come and work for us?"

I'm not sure what to say and look at Martha, who shakes

her head and looks at me pointedly, warning me against saying anything.

"I'm happy here, honey. Despite what you think, I will never leave your mom. She will need me more than ever now, so don't you worry about me and just go and be happy. Make sure you come back and visit though, I will want to hear all the details."

As they hug it out, Martha winks at me over Angel's shoulder. I wonder if she will ever tell Angel and Anastasia who she really is. It's obvious she's not ready for that yet, but I don't know why.

As we turn and say our goodbyes, I take Angel's hand in mine and as the door closes behind us, I stop and say softly, "I always imagined leaving this house one day with your hand in mine. I imagined us leaving to set up life together and now it's coming true."

Angel nods. "It's a strange feeling leaving the past behind. For a while there, I thought this would never happen but now it has, everything makes sense again."

She turns and my arms wrap round her and pull her tightly against me. As we share a kiss on the steps of her childhood home, I take a moment to remember her father. He was hard, unforgiving and a bastard and between us we broke the beauty who now trembles in my arms. However, it was done for a reason and now I understand why; it built us both into stronger people because now we appreciate what we have and can handle what life throws at us together as a strong team. Ultimately, it's made us stronger together than we ever were apart and the cunning old fox can sleep soundly in the afterlife knowing that his plan worked out in the end. Harvey's girls are strong women, and now it's time for Anastasia to prove to us all just what she's made of.

Angel pulls away and smiles, "Come on, we have a wedding to attend."

She laughs and I swear it lights up the darkness that approaches with the passing of the day and as we walk hand in hand into our future, I know it will be a good one because she's by my side.

※

CARRY on reading **Owning Beauty**

I like to own the best that money can buy.
I like to surround myself with beauty and Art. I want the best and don't care how far I go to own it.
She's about to discover that I always go a step too far.
She gave up everything to be my wife but there is still one valuable asset she owns that causes the feral beast in me to growl.

Her innocence.

My world is a dark and dangerous place full of nightmares that never go away.
My beauty is about to wake up and discover the prince who rescued her from the tower is a beast in disguise and she will hear me roar as I claim the innocence of my virgin bride.

Yes, I can live without love but I can't live without that and nothing is going to stand in my way because what Tobias Moretti wants – he gets, over and over again.

If you enjoyed Breaking Beauty, please would you be so kind as to leave a review on Amazon?

Join my closed Facebook Group

Stella's Sexy Readers

Follow me on Instagram

Stay healthy and happy and thanks for reading xx

Carry on reading for more Reaper Romances, Mafia Romance & more.

Remember to grab your free copy of The Highest Bidder by visiting stellaandrews.com.

BOOKS BY STELLA ANDREWS

Twisted Reapers

Sealed With a Broken Kiss
Dirty Hero (Snake & Bonnie)
Daddy's Girls (Ryder & Ashton)
Twisted (Sam & Kitty)
The Billion Dollar baby (Tyler & Sydney)
Bodyguard (Jet & Lucy)
Flash (Flash & Jennifer)
Country Girl (Tyson & Sunny)

The Romanos
The Throne of Pain (Lucian & Riley)
The Throne of Hate (Dante & Isabella)
The Throne of Fear (Romeo & Ivy)
Lorenzo's story is in Broken Beauty

Beauty Series
Breaking Beauty (Sebastian & Angel) *
Owning Beauty (Tobias & Anastasia)
Broken Beauty (Maverick & Sophia) *
Completing Beauty – The series

Five Kings

Catch a King (Sawyer & Millie) *

<u>Slade</u>

Steal a King

Break a King

Destroy a King

Marry a King

Baron

Club Mafia

Club Mafia – The Contract

Club Mafia – The Boss

Club Mafia – The Angel

Club Mafia – The Savage

Standalone

The Highest Bidder (Logan & Samantha)

Rocked (Jax & Emily)

Brutally British

Deck the Boss

Reasons to sign up to my mailing list.

- A reminder that you can read my books FREE with Kindle Unlimited.
- Receive a monthly newsletter so you don't miss out on any special offers or new releases.
- Links to follow me on Amazon or social media to be kept up to date with new releases.
- Free books and bonus content.
- Opportunities to read my books before they are even released by

joining my team.

•Sneak peeks at new material before anyone else.

stellaandrews.com

Follow me on Amazon

Printed in Great Britain
by Amazon